Footprints of A Legend

Bitterroot Series

Russell Victor Acord

Dedication

I want to thank Vic for all the words of encouragement and direction through the years it took to finish this first book. Not only have you been a great example and mentor, you have always been the person I looked to for answers. I would expect nothing less from my father. Dad, I dedicate this book to you.

Special Thank You

There is always a story behind the success of a long term project such as writing a novel. I appreciate the encouragement by several family members and friends to finish my story and put it out there to share with others. I want to especially thank my wife, Lori, who always put the boots to the appropriate part of my anatomy to keep my writing moving forward. Over the years you have pulled and pushed me through the most difficult pages of my life and the toughest chapters of this book. Without your help and constant cheering this first book would have stayed locked away in my mind and the words would have never made it to the following pages. With my deepest love and gratitude; I thank you, and I love you!

Footprints of A Legend

A Novel By

Russell Victor Acord

Acknowledgment

I would like express that I couldn't have made the connection of the face I saw in my mind's eye without the masterful art of Pam McKee. This exceptional artist grew up as my childhood friend and neighbor in Florence Montana, not far from Kootenai Mountain, the backdrop of this entire story. Pam's artwork has given our readers a face to put with the Legend that's had us all wondering for so many years.

Thank You Pamela!

Forward

The time line of this book is based in 2007 when the forest fires of Montana were burning hot and the wildlife was pushed into the low lands or deeper into the wilderness to escape the smoke and fire. Currently there are two more books being written to carry the adventure into today's time-line and put into perspective the preceding events to 2007.

If you enjoy the following pages and the adventure that you are about to embark on, please by all means let your friends know where to find this novel. I am self published and my success is largely decided by the readers who appreciate my efforts and share their enjoyment by word of mouth. Thank you for your interest in the Footprints of a Legend series. I hope you enjoy this novel as much as I have enjoyed writing it.

Chapter Index

Bitter Roots

I grew up as a great wilderness enthusiast and big game hunter in the Bitterroot Mountains of Montana. At an early age, I understood that the wilderness needs to be respected as well as protected due to the rough terrain and fragile life within. As a young boy my father would take me into the high country through rockslides and heavily wooded areas where he would point out different tracks of the wildlife that inhabited the beautiful landscape. Each day provided a new lesson in outdoor survival. Fishing trips and camping in the never ending beauty had grown to be my favorite pastime. Little did I know that the lessons I learned in those backcountry wilderness trips, was an education for my survival in the future. It was here in the Bitterroot Mountain Range of Montana, high up on Kootenai Mountain, where the following journey begins.

I was 33 years old with seven years of military service in the US Army behind me. I was feeling the need to get out and reunite myself with my childhood. I wanted some high-altitude exercise, and a little reflection with time to drink up the plentiful supply of the pure fresh mountain air. Over the past several years I had seen my share of the military "action" and desperately needed some time alone in the wild for a bit of self healing and a lot less background noise. Nothing in my military career or my experience with the wilderness could have prepared me for the mysterious and wild events that lie ahead.

It was mid August of 2007 and the wide-spread smoke from the distant forest fires had the Bitterroot Valley looking hazed and appearing overcast. There had been no rain to speak of and summer was clearly going to continue its pattern of warm nights and hot, dry days.

A few years ago my parents sold our old farmhouse on the eastside highway in Florence and moved to some acreage in Helena, Montana. Trying to keep up with the livestock and ranch in Florence was too much for my parents without help. So I wouldn't be able to drop in unannounced and stay with them like I had in the past. I felt a little cheated as Mom always made the best breakfast in town and the familiar shuffling of Dad's morning newspaper was something that I had missed over the years. I checked in at a local hotel in Stevensville instead, just minutes away from the Kootenai Mountain trailhead. I prepared my backpack for a five or six day trip into the steep, rugged mountains and felt my anticipation grow. I was excited to get out, explore my old stomping grounds and fish the fresh backcountry streams for some rainbow trout. I knew I could make a fishing pole out of available branches or saplings so I stopped by the old convenience store in Florence and picked out a few fishing flies that were sure to catch the Moby Dick of the high country. I put three flies inside my wallet and hooked three more on the rim of my tattered baseball cap. I bought a disposable camera, beef jerky and picked out a couple of cheap lighters for *campfires made easy.* I laughed to myself as I thought of my military training on how to make fire without the benefit of matches or lighters. Boy was I going to be spoiled on this trip! I picked up a small spool of fishing line to complete my fishing supplies for the trip and headed south on highway 93 towards Stevensville.

I woke up around four-thirty in the morning and reviewed the list of necessary items needed for the trip and finished tightening up my backpack. After a half cup of awful tasting instant hotel coffee, I pulled on my good old trusty handcrafted Whites boots and headed for the truck. I backed out of the parking lot and looked up at the majestic

Kootenai Mountain. I felt a great sense of calmness as I took in the view and contours of the beautiful Bitterroot Mountain Range. The hint of the red sunrise offered a nice backdrop for the jagged edges of the cliffs and mountain as it erupted skyward into the fading stars. Before I drove too far, I called Dad on the cell phone to give him a heads up on what I was up to.

"Howdy Son," Dad said.

"Hey mister, how goes it?" I asked.

"Oh, you know how it is, heading out to feed the horses and irritate the dog. What are you doing up this early?"

"I'm in the Bitterroot Valley heading up to Kootenai for a week or so and see if our old stomping grounds have changed any. When was the last time you were up there?" I inquired.

"Well, I guess last year Jeff and I went elk hunting up on the summit. Don't you worry son, it hasn't changed much and it's all still tough and still beautiful," Dad replied.

Jeff was dad's favorite hunting buddy; the two always seemed to find a tougher climb and more challenging terrain to conquer every year. He had enjoyed Jeff's company and the two would constantly find some kind of trouble in the woods together, claiming that trouble had found them. Growing up in the Bitterroot Valley, Jeff seemed to be a natural part of the scenery. He was the picture perfect mountain man with great stories of adventure from deep within the backcountry. He struck me as one of those guys who had been born a hundred years too late, missing his calling as a mountain fur trader. There was always a gleam in his eye when he told stories of a new cliff or basin full of wildlife that he discovered in the wild mountainous country. He would always begin his adventure stories with:

And there I was, smoking gun in each hand, both chambers empty and out of bullets with my back against the wall, lying there in the dirt in front of me was a dead, riddled full of holes... tin can.

I guess since I was out seeing the rest of the world, dad and Jeff kept this neck of the woods under close observation. Jeff's broad smile matched his broad shoulders and thick black hair, I never saw the man without feeling a touch of envy for all the time he spent in the woods and the carefree spirit that surrounded him.

"Well," I said, "I'm going to follow the creek up the main trail for a couple of miles, break away to the right and set up a dry camp on the backside of the summit where we used to stay."

"Sounds like a good time but be careful with the fire because you know how quickly conditions can change," Dad advised. "Give me a call when you get back down and we'll grab a bite to eat at Ruby's Café in Missoula. I'll even pay for it this time."

"Sounds great, I'll give you a call you in about a week. Love you Dad," I said.

"Love you too, Son," Dad hung up.

The morning air was cool, but you could tell it would be warm soon. I needed to hit the trail early and begin my climb while there was still some shade left in the canyon. Once I left the trail I would be on that east side with the hot sun. After parking my truck and hiding my keys on the truck body, I took a short pause at the trailhead to take in the clean air before heading up the steep Kootenai trail towards higher ground. The rushing water on the left side of the trail was loud and comforting as I began my morning hike with the jagged cliffs looming above to my right. What a great feeling after being away for so long. Dad was right, it felt new to me but everything was still familiar and very much the same. After about forty-five minutes, I came to a wide area where I could step off the main trail and begin my tough climb up the mountainside to the right. The sound of the rushing water had faded away as I came up the trail and separated from the stream down in the bottom of the canyon. The climb up the side of the mountain was much steeper and a little slower going. After a couple hours of hard climbing I turned away from the mountain and looked back down through the canyon and out across the hazy Bitterroot Valley. I felt pride as the beauty of the steep mountain fell away into the vast range of the peaceful valley below. Wow, this truly was God's country! The valley far below looked like a velvet blanket of green tones as they rolled gently into the dark trees that covered the more aggressive terrain of the mountains that blocked out the breathtaking blue skyline.

When I turned back up the hill, three mule deer headed away from me on the next ridge with their oversized ears perked, and their hard hooves crunching the steep, rocky ground. I hadn't seen any wildlife in so long. The sighting was familiar but exciting to see deer in their natural element again. I watched in awe as they moved effortlessly through the difficult terrain and disappeared quickly over the hilltop. As I caught my breath and continued up the incline, it occurred to me that it would be great to have had my father here with me. He climbed these mountains like a Billy goat and always made me feel as if I were holding him up. Dad would stop and wait for me on the trail ahead with that big confident smile of his. He was conditioned for this kind of climbing and could cover a tremendous amount of territory during hunting season. If anything would have made this trip any better, it would have been having him here with me. I sure missed his company.

As I reached the summit, the wind picked up and the air turned cooler. The view below was hazy, but still amazing. On one side was the beautiful Bitterroot Valley and on the other was the wild and wonderful Bitterroot Mountain ranges reaching far off into Idaho. This is just what I needed... rugged wild country with no cell phones, traffic, interruptions or deadlines. I was finally alone, surrounded by nothing but beauty and open space with free time to absorb as much fresh air as possible over the next few days. I dropped over the ridgeline, a few hundred feet from view of the Bitterroot Valley and looked over the heavily wooded mountainside beyond.

I continued along below the ridge looking for place to set up camp.   Within a half hour I found the perfect flat spot below a small rockslide. Nestled within a cluster of smaller trees and shrubs was a nice big pine for support and protection from the breeze. I had a grand view of the backside of Kootenai Mountain and the vast rugged range towards Idaho that seemed to go on forever in front of me.

I tied off my five foot by eight foot tarp, broke off several green pine boughs, and made a nice comfortable bed to sleep the night away. I tossed my rolled sleeping bag on top. I dug through my backpack and picked out some dried mangos and beef jerky. There was a breeze blowing so I decided not to build a fire tonight. The temperature was plenty warm enough anyway. Drinking water from my canteen, I tried to take in the whole scene—the trees, cliffs, mountains, wildlife and the sweet presence of nature all around me. I was away from all the hustle and bustle of civilization. This is what I would call "living it up." It was starting to get late, and I wasn't surprised at how tired I was from the day's challenging climb. I rested my backpack against the tree as a pillow and prepared to lay out my light-weight sleeping bag.

Kneeling down to unlace my boots, I heard what sounded like two rocks scraping together, as if something was crossing over the rockslide area above my camp. I figured it was another mule deer but I didn't want to miss out on seeing more wildlife so I had to take a peek. I sneaked around the big pine tree and dropped down so I could keep a little cover between myself and the rocks above. Once I was about fifty feet away, I headed back up the trail retracing my ear-lier steps and approached the opening. From this vantage point I had a full view of the rocky area above my camp. Suddenly I was engulfed by a terrible stench! It was like I had walked into a cloud of skunk spray, only this was much worse. I had never smelled anything like this in my life. Could it be a bear had been eating something rotten? Or maybe there was a gut pile from something left behind? It smelled of a wet dog that had just vomited up rancid meat it had just eaten, only much more potent. (I knew that smell compliments of my old Golden Labrador during hunting season).

Just as quickly as it came, the obvious odor was gone, and from what I could tell there was nothing to see in the opening. Not even the pesky chattering squirrel that had scolded me earlier as I passed by. In fact, there was no movement at all. There wasn't even the background sound of chirping birds, chipmunks or even the wind. I felt the hair on the back of my neck start to rise.

"Oh *I don't like this feeling at all",* I whispered out loud.

Was there a bear, mountain lion, or possibly even a wolf hanging around? I knew there was an occasional bear in these areas and periodically wolves will also hunt this mountain range. I knew I had better stay alert and keep the old .45 pistol close. Heading back towards camp, I kept my left hand on my pistol for comfort. I felt like a wide-eyed owl looking for anything that might be out of place. I knew the wilderness is always full of surprises and should not be taken for granted. I had to be watchful and not become dinner for a hungry meat eater.

Out of nowhere the terrible odor struck my nose again. The stench combined with the forest's silence had the hair on my neck tingling straight up. Something was watching me—I could feel it.

Alright, I told myself, *I'm an armed military man in the woods and have no problem using my weapon. I can handle this. I'm a big boy and I am not going to be worried about some nasty smell in the dark.*

I knew this mountain belonged to the wildlife, and I was the uninvited guest. Maybe coming out to this mountain was a bad idea. Perhaps I was in the wrong place at the wrong time. Darkness was descending and the shadows were looking a little less friendly. It was time to get the flashlight ready and set myself up for a restless night. Wow! What was that nasty smell coming and going? Unfamiliar smells in the wilderness are not unusual but this odor seemed to stop the forest dead and leave a spooky silence in the air. Usually the birds and night sounds have a calming effect that helps me drift off to sleep, but tonight was stone quiet and felt completely unfriendly. The evening wind had stopped and left an unsettling heavy tension blanketing the night. The rancid smell was strong and almost nauseating with a pungent odor of unknown sweat and stench. Elk and deer have their own distinctive, unattractive smell, and even the bear doesn't smell this bad. This particular odor had me stumped!

Everything had come to a complete stop in the forest. The overwhelming sense that something was watching me had become too evident to ignore. I wondered if I should put my pack together and move on to another camp site, or even leave this side of the summit. Heading back to the trailhead was out of the question, as there was no way I could navigate such rough terrain in the dark without serious risk. Maybe I could drop down to the cliff area and back myself into a rocky spot with only one point of entry? At least that way I could limit my approach of unwanted visitors. It would be better to close up my vulnerable sides to a smaller range. Whatever was out there wasn't going to have the advantage of coming from any direction it wanted. I decided I needed to move so I could protect myself if necessary.

This was a good plan. Make the tactical decision by getting into a strong point and hold my position for the night. I pulled my tarp down and started wrapping it up. Out of the corner of my eye, I caught a flicker of movement. Was it really movement or was I starting to get myself worked up? It was dark enough now that I wasn't certain, so I kept working. I stood up and looked towards the rocky area and saw what appeared to be someone standing maybe two hundred feet away. I couldn't be sure though since the shadows were long. All the hairs on my body stood at attention and my palms began to sweat. My unease was intense! What was the big deal and why was I being so paranoid?

If someone was out there maybe they don't know what to think of me either.

"Hello?" I called out. Nothing moved. I froze and stood still, hearing only the sound of my own heartbeat in the silence.

The smell was really powerful now. There was still no movement from the odd shape above me. Maybe it was an old tree stump that I hadn't noticed before or a dark shadow in the rocks playing tricks on me. The frozen silence and strong smell hung thick in the air.

"Mister, you seriously need a bubble bath!" I laughed out loud.

Hearing my words out loud seemed funny and somehow made me feel a little better. I brushed my hand across my pistol. Knowing it was close and loaded was comforting. Yet, the awful smell and the disturbing shadow still had me uneasy. I stood quietly for a moment, peering into the night, giving special attention to the odd dark shadow above my camp. I didn't want to use my light as I began putting things into my pack. I wanted my eyes to stay acclimated to the darkness.

The light crack of a rock grinding on another broke the silence and confirmed I was not alone. I stopped moving and stood completely still with all senses on high alert. I strained my eyes and ears to get the exact location of where the noise had come. It was so close! The heavy smell was all around me, enveloping me like a second skin. My eyes pierced the darkness for any movement or indication as to what was out there. I took a step forward and moved closer to the large pine tree and slid my pistol from its holster, drawing the hammer back, and holding it low. I carefully scanned from the right to the left, until my eyes made their way back up to where the odd dark shadow was above my camp. It was gone!

Every hair on my body was standing straight up and the saliva in my mouth vanished leaving it dry and tasteless. My pounding heart was going to erupt out of my chest, and the sound of my own breathing seemed loud and hollow as I tried to control my emotions. I was certain every creature in the wilderness could hear the adrenaline pulsing through my body on this quiet, eerie night. Every ounce of my being was caught in this terrifying moment as the seconds seemed to slow down to an agonizing pace. I cautiously shifted my weight to look back downhill, with my pistol held low in front of me. Not more than twenty feet away from me stood what looked to be a large bear standing on its hind legs. Something was very odd with the scene in front of me. In the darkness it was coming towards me on its hind legs, like a man. Quickly I raised my pistol to make sure I had the upper hand, but I was much too late. Before I realized what was happening, I was slammed with my back into the large pine tree directly behind me. The solid tree smashed into my flesh and cut deep against my back bone and ribs. The speed in which this animal covered the distance was unnatural and ferocious.

As my shoulder struck the tree, I felt the pistol jump in my hands as it fired low into the body that rammed me. The force of the blow sent the pistol spinning into the darkness. The massive size of this animal made me feel like a mere infant at its mercy. The pungent smell was sickening as I felt my stomach heave. I felt myself falling, my body bouncing off the pine. I plunged forward and came down hard with my face on a large flat rock at the base of the tree. The shocking taste of my own blood from biting through my upper lip frightened me. I knew the smell of my blood would only encourage the aggression if this beast was a flesh eating animal.

Without a sound, the creature was instantly on me again with superhuman strength and power, yet with the human hands of a large man. Was this a gorilla, or a man, a freak of nature escaped from a zoo? What the heck was happening to me? As the enormous hands grabbed my right arm and left thigh, I was picked up with virtually no effort and pitched to the ground with incredible force. As I landed, I remember putting out my hands to catch myself, but the force was too great and the ground accepted me with a tremendous thud. My face hit the exposed roots of the large pine tree splitting open my cheek just under my left eye. Oh please, I thought, let me become unconscious before this thing tries to eat me! I couldn't bear the thought of hearing the sounds of my own bones being crushed by this monster. Once I hit the ground, everything was still, nothing moved. The beast was standing over me and breathing so close that I could feel the hot rancid breath on the side of my bleeding face.

Be still, I told myself. *Play dead, maybe it will lose interest and go away.*

After waiting for what seemed like an eternity the large hands wrapped themselves around my arm and thigh again, pulling me out and away from the tree. Was this where it was going to pull me apart and feed on me? Is this how it was all going to end?

"No!" I yelled.

Using every bit of strength I possessed I tried to break away from its rock-hard grip.

I may as well have been trying to lift a full sized pickup truck. The strength and size of this creature was easily a few hundred pounds heavier than me. Kicking with all my might as I tried to free myself, I was lifted high up off the ground and again thrust towards the unforgiving earth. Thankfully all went black.

As I regained consciousness, I became aware that the earth was flying by, literally. I was rushing through the woods on the shoulders of what felt like an enormous man. My head was spinning, and I had lost a fair amount of blood as it was still flowing from my face. My body was draped over the creature's shoulder like a rag doll, my face bouncing off of its back, and the same sickening smell penetrating my nostrils. Its back was broad and hot with sweat oozing from its surface confirming that this was not a costume but a live creature with more strength and power than I had ever encountered in my life. I thought this had to be a form of human carrying me, as nothing else walked upright and had humanlike hands.

I thought about the old tales of the legendary Bigfoot, or Sasquatch, that had been told around the campfires to scare the living daylights out of children. Yeah right, Bigfoot! There's no such thing. It's only a great imagination growing into tall tales of something that doesn't exist.

Every inch of my body ached, and I couldn't feel my legs anymore. The numbness was probably due to the lack of circulation from being carried like a toy doll. I made the mistake of trying to adjust myself or maybe even get some leverage to break away from the grip of this monster. In an instant, the thing effortlessly hoisted me up high, and I heard the wind rush past my ears as I came crashing back down to the earth. Darkness closed in on me again.

Through the haze between blackouts I heard the sounds of running water, rocks, gravel and even branches and brush that tugged at my clothing. Was I back on the other side of Kootenai Mountain again? Where were we going in such haste? What does this monster want with me, this beast who kept me sedated by bouncing me off the ground like a ball? I needed it to be over so I could be free from all the pain pulsing throughout my face and battered body. As I checked in and out of consciousness, I could tell I was in a large body of water, not really swimming, but rather being carried through deep, still water and submerging my captor to its chest. I saw a hint of the morning sunrise coming in from the east and then blackness again.

Wake Up Call

When I woke, I was painfully aware of the throbbing in my head, face, back and down both legs, but everything was still. I'm assuming it was from the game of "throw the camper to the ground or bounce him off the nearest tree" the night before. I opened my right eye and found that my left eye was swollen completely shut. Focusing my right eye on my surroundings, I could see the sun was high in the sky, and the warmth was like a comfortable blanket on my body. From my vantage point, I was lying flat on a rock, with my head facing uphill. There were absolutely no sounds, and even the wind was still. I propped myself on my elbow to see more and could sense that I was not alone. I felt the eyes of something very close, intently watching my every move. I turned my head and saw the knees and oversized bare feet of what looked like a really hairy athlete. Startled, I sat up into a sitting position for a better look at whom or what was above me. As I turned all the way around, I beheld a six-foot tall creature standing there, curiously looking back at me. His ears protruded straight out from his head as if they were being pulled by two hands.

His body reminded me of a gorilla at the zoo with his black and brown hair that was nearly two to three inches long, yet he had the facial features of a man with a slightly longer forehead. He stood upright on two feet just like a human, though his hands and feet seemed to be too big for his body. I stared at him in disbelief. *This little pipsqueak couldn't be the same monster that man handled me the night before could it?* What I encountered the previous night seemed much taller, truly massive, and bulky compared to me. Could it be that there was more than one of these freaks of nature out here in the wild? Looking him over, I saw this was a very stout animal for its size with the physique of a bodybuilder with strong, bulging arms that were longer and somewhat larger than my own. His eyes looked young and wide with fearlessness in his gaze. His chin was square and strong with a mouth that turned down at the sides. For no more than six feet tall, the thought of agitating him still seemed like a really bad idea. He stared back at me with interest and a mild inquisitiveness. The facial expression was oddly enough, very much human.

What did this thing want with me? Was I going to be the next thing on the menu? Sitting there staring at this creature I began to wonder what kind of animal this was. Was the legend of Bigfoot real? With the large feet and hands, hairy body, and standing on two feet like a man, it all seemed to add up to the campfire stories of Sasquatch. The thought of there really being such a beast in the woods had always come across as a big joke. This particular joke was living, foul smelling, and looking back at me with dark, piercing eyes.

For some reason, I didn't feel any immediate threat from this six-foot male standing in front of me. He had an almost friendly, calm appearance as he stood there casually but still alert. His overall presence might not be aggressive right now, but I knew I really didn't want to provoke him either.

We were in what appeared to be the center of a huge rockslide area. There was a small strip of earth in the middle where the rocks had settled around a high ridge of ground which protruded out of the slide. The open area was about five acres wide and covered in bear grass, a few medium size trees and some boulders on the upper side of the clearing. Beyond that, in all directions were large rocks from a rockslide many years ago. There seemed to be nothing else in sight except for me and my odd companion in the clearing. Past the clearing were several distant mountain ranges that didn't look familiar. Was it possible this animal in front of me could be responsible for all the chaos and trauma from the night before? Was I so excited that in my mind I exaggerated the size and strength of this thing or was this furry beast truly larger than life?

I slowly and painfully moved from my sitting position to a kneeling position directly facing my companion to help the blood flow back into my legs. His eyes went from curious and relaxed, to watchful and alert and could not be mistaken for anything but ready for battle. With my hands on the ground in front of me for stability, I kept still, trying to keep from losing my balance and never taking my eyes off the creature in front of me. My body hurt and ached, as if I had been in a terrible car wreck. My eye was tight from the swelling and my upper lip felt like I had bitten it all the way through in more than one spot. The center of my back was bleeding and my shoulder was tight with swelling. I really didn't want any more rough play from anyone, especially this tough looking hairball with the protruding potato head ears in front of me.

I knew I didn't want to appear aggressive or threatening, so I lowered my gaze back down to the ground and then out toward the open clearing and rocks beyond. Unsure of where I was, I did realize that I was a long way from where I had set up camp the previous night. The terrain was much rougher and there was a glacier off to the right, not more than five hundred yards away. In all directions there were majestic rough mountain ranges, which meant that I was so far in the back country that there would be no trails for me to recognize. I had no idea if I was in Idaho or Montana. Quite simply, I was so lost that I wouldn't have a clue as to which direction to go or even the strength to get too far even if I wanted to.

I noticed my companion looking towards the glacier and appeared to be getting a little anxious. As I followed his gaze, I was surprised to see what looked to be two larger versions of the beast heading across the clearing towards us about two hundred yards away. I'm not sure where they had come from because I could have sworn we were all alone. The two walked tall, like two men strolling side by side with the same arm-swinging stride, only these two were much larger than the one directly in front of me. I could see that even at this distance. As they came closer, I saw the one on the left had a distinct red tone to his hair color, and the other walked with a limp in his stride, favoring his right leg. Clearly these two were adults and the one in front of me was more of an adolescent.

The sheer size of the two newcomers was frightening and intimidating as the look on their faces was so human-like and not friendly. The one with the limp had a long, bulging scar on the right side of his face that ran the entire length from his brow through his eye all the way to his jaw line. His overall appearance was very confident with strong shoulders, oversized forearms and massive chest. He looked like a terrifying, battle-seasoned warrior with a flat nose that looked like it had been broken many times. His shoulders were sloped and massive with upper arms more than twice as big around as my thighs. The hands of the three subjects were all oversized and thick by proportion and looked as though they could crush a skull with little or no effort.

The one with the red tint to its hair had very small eyes that seemed cruel and cut through you as they stared you down. He looked as if he would be one that would pull you apart with his huge hands, eat you for lunch then pick his teeth with your rib. Of the two adults, he was slightly smaller in height than the other by maybe one or two inches, but thicker throughout his overall body. I would guess him to be about seven and a half feet tall, roughly three hundred and seventy five pounds or better. Either way, I knew this was not the time to aggravate or test them in any way. The one with the slight limp stepped forward, put his massive hand on my right shoulder and gripped firmly as he easily pulled me to my feet. Without letting go he hesitated, looking down into my face with frightening intensity, piercing right through me. He glanced down at his own right hip which was caked with dried blood. The other, with the red tint to his color walked around behind me and stood quietly out of my view, solidifying my helpless predicament. Was this going to be the end of the trail for me? I started feeling sick to my stomach as the powerful odor of these two surrounded me.

The youngster turned and started walking towards the glacier and the one with the iron clad grip turned me towards the glacier and pushed me in behind him. Clearly I was going to follow the youngest of the three. My body screamed with pain at the sudden activity. My legs were so stiff that it was difficult to walk, let alone keep up with the stride of these taller hosts.

As we walked along, I noticed with my one good eye that the younger one in front of me had something tied to both of his feet, almost like sandals. I saw that he had several small branches entangled with dried up fur tied to the bottom of each foot. Did these guys really wear shoes for protection on their feet and where did they ever get the idea to do such a thing?

When I looked down at my own feet, I was grateful for the boots I had on for protection and warmth. I looked in the dirt to see what tracks he had left behind. There was nothing but undistinguishable smudges in the ground, no track at all. It was absolutely brilliant! How could you track an animal that left no identifying marks on the ground? Was I really here and seeing this? Was this truly a face to face experience with the legendary Bigfoot?

The younger guide turned abruptly and headed uphill towards the rockslide. I didn't know how far we were going, but I knew in my condition I would have a tough time navigating the steep rocks ahead. I watched the young beast step up into the rocks and simply disappear. He never emerged on the rocks ahead! As I climbed up onto the same rock face, I saw an opening of a cave down below. The mouth of the cave was roughly four feet high by six feet wide and very well hidden. It could only be seen from above the opening itself. The red male abruptly stopped me and pushed me hard into a seated position. I felt the blood rush back into my upper body and the numbing pain really kicked in. Did he have to be so heavy handed?

The red colored male stayed behind as the larger one brushed past me and quickly ducked into the opening. I stayed still, facing the opening and felt the little eyes of the red beast boring a hole in my back. His breathing was loud and heavy and his smell was awful as it permeated the area. I turned slightly and kept my eyes down so I could see his feet. Sure enough, he had several pine boughs with fur secured to his massive foot with what appeared to be leather from an animal skin or gut. I began to realize that these creatures didn't want to be noticed or tracked down, but how did they learn to hide their existence so well and for so long? From deep within the cave I heard the sounds of heavy dragging, like a team working together to move a heavy object.

Light footsteps approached the opening of the cave, but stopped just short of view and a loud, throaty cough bellowed once from inside the opening. Instantly the footsteps scurried away, taking with them the sound similar to that of a child who taunts "Plbbbbbt" at a playmate. Only this time it was not funny but scary and unfamiliar. I had no idea what was in store or how many of these creatures were there and what had made the odd sounds within the deep black cave.

I got the feeling this smelly cave was no where I wanted to be with God knows what inside of it. The sounds were frightening and not knowing what lie ahead was making me seriously uncomfortable. Were these creatures getting ready to have me for supper? Is this how life was going to end for me, in this smelly cave? I still had my Leatherman on my belt and a single lighter in my right pocket. My wallet was in my left hip pocket and a small spool of fishing line was bulging from my left front pocket. The only other thing I had was my wrist-watch and my military dog tags that hung from my neck. Against these odds and in my current condition I was not at all prepared to defend myself or escape with my limited tools or weapons, especially under such close observation.

Another set of footsteps approached the entrance and the younger male with the pro-truding ears came out through the opening. Without a sound, the large male behind me brushed by and disappeared into the opening leaving the young male standing there look-ing at me. He seemed odd with his large ears and beady dark eyes, but not nearly as scary as the other two. He seemed curious about my black wristwatch and couldn't keep his gaze off of it.

As I watched him, he looked kind of goofy in a way with his extra long arms, big, exag-gerated hands and radar ears. I bet with those ears he could hear a squirrel fart a thousand yards away. The thought made me smile and quietly laugh out loud, which startled my big-eared friend, causing him to step backwards on the steep rock and lose his footing on the smooth surface. He started falling and flailing his big, clumsy arms trying to regain his balance. In his effort to keep from crashing down, his leg flew up with such speed that his makeshift shoe flew off and hit me in the stomach. His impressive, heavy footed high kick threw his balance so out of control that the fight against gravity put him upside down on his back and shoulders with a loud thud. The steep smooth surface had him sliding downward where only his head disappeared into the opening of the cave. The sight of this huge furry beast on his back, lying upside down and his big feet pointing towards the sky before me was entirely too much to hold it together. I burst out in uncontrollable laughter!

In a flash, my young friend was back on his feet looking truly humiliated, searching for his long lost shoe. I nudged it towards him with my toe as the tears of laughter continued streaming down my face. The large male appeared at the cave's entrance, and the agitated look on his face was easy enough for both of us to read. Immediately we became still, quiet and respectful. Fighting back the tears and laughter was difficult, but necessary. Seeing his expression was sobering, but what he held was much more interesting and disturbing.

In his oversized hands was a book. It was a kind of notebook that one might use to write a diary. It looked very old and well used with a tattered canvas cover and big bold faded writing on its front. The thought of these guys being able to read seemed farfetched. I could only see the first two letters which read 'LT' written in black ink. With a quick bark from the large male, my companion quickly replaced his shoe and stood up straight. He quickly and quietly disappeared back into the cave. My head was spinning from everything I had taken in: the notebook, the makeshift sandals, these creatures. How did these beasts come to possess this notebook? I was dizzy from the sight and smell of the nasty creatures and the obvious damage to my body. I hoped this was all just a twisted dream and I would soon wake up in my own camp on the backside of Kootenai Mountain.

We sat there for about an hour and a half with intermittent appearances from the two adult males until the larger of the two males finally came out and stood towering in front of me. His eyes looked tired and worried as he ushered me back down the rocks toward the glacier. Taking the lead, the large male with the scar on his face limped forward. My young friend followed close behind as we quietly walked towards the icy blue glacier beyond the clearing. As I followed the large male, I knew I would have to come to terms with the fact that this was indeed, the legendary Bigfoot and I was in the middle of its habitat.

He was a tremendous creature with the build of a great athlete and almost the size of Andre the Giant. His limp looked as if he was favoring his right leg and it seemed to be giving him a little trouble. What startled me was the fresh gash about six inches long, on the top of his right pelvic bone. Recalling the night before, I remembered my pistol firing when I was hit. Perhaps this was the intruder I had shot the night before and had only grazed his hip. The gash looked pretty bad with a fairly large tear where the bullet had made its exit. I couldn't believe this was the beast that had carried me through the night and covered so much territory with such an injury.

Bed and Breakfast

I was so focused on the incredible beast in front of me that I hadn't noticed the old log cabin in front of me until I had almost run into the side of it. It appeared to be an old trapper's cabin from a very long time ago, with a roof that seemed to still be intact. The structure had no door to speak of and the openings for the windows were closed up with shutters made of tightly woven branches and rawhide. My host stopped and stepped to the side, as if to encourage me to continue inside. Slowly, I put my hand on the doorway and cautiously stepped one foot inside the dry, musty interior and stopped.

It was fairly dark inside, but I only stepped inside far enough to see what my giant friend would do. Quietly he stood there, blankly looking into the doorway at me with a look of impatience. After a short hesitation, he turned and walked away towards the cave. The younger male lingered just outside the doorway and watched me, curious to see what I would do next. The larger male stopped about fifty feet away and looked back at the younger male and waited. When the youth realized that the larger male was impatiently waiting, he turned around and moved quickly towards the adult.

The two continued out of sight and into the rocks of the hidden cave. Without moving my feet, I waited a moment to let my eyes adjust to the dark interior of the cabin. To my surprise, the cabin was divided in half by a short wall, the side on the left had a wooden bed frame with sturdy looking branches lying across for support and strips of skin tied from side to side. An old blanket and several other cloth items were all bunched up on the floor beside the bed. The half on the right had a small, weak shelf with miscellaneous items scattered about, and a sturdy chair lying on its side made from thick branches that had been tied together. Close to the door was a rickety old table that looked as if it would crumble in with very little effort. There were two wooden boxes on the floor behind the table, one which had several items inside and the other was empty and broken.

Was this my new bed and breakfast of the Wild West Inn, or was this going to be my new prison? Why had I been plucked out of the mountains and brought to this remote place? I couldn't imagine the thought of spending the cold winter months in this tired old cabin without a few trips to the building supply store. The overall appearance of the interior wasn't too bad for its age. For an old structure, it had been well maintained by someone. As I scanned the room with the bed, I noticed the bed wasn't as old as the cabin. This piece of furniture was a recent addition, as it was tethered together with some wire and several pieces of string or rawhide and looked solid. Who had occupied this building before my arrival? The blanket on the floor was an old green wool Army blanket that had seen better days, but was still useable. The other items on the bed were two pairs of men's pants and several rough looking shirts that had been well worn and stitched together many times.

Dirty, sore, and exhausted the thought of lying down on that bed was too much to resist. I moved the clothes away and rolled the blanket up for a pillow and sat on the edge of the bed wondering, who was the last to occupy this building and where was that person today? I stretched out my sore legs and lay back on the wooden bed and looked up at the ceiling. Hanging from one of the support beams was a small pouch, about the size of a cigarette pack. Intrigued, I stood up and carefully pulled it down drawing the strings apart to see inside.

I reached in and pulled out five bullets that were green and black from moisture and a piece of broken mirror. Also inside was a piece of thick paper. Pulling it out I saw that it was an old black and white photo folded in half: "Kapowsin, WA. Dempsy Labor Co. with Frank and Paul, 1909" was all it said on the back. Being careful not to tear the paper I cautiously opened the old photo. It was a portrait of a young man in his early 20's standing beside a large, freshly cut log that was a good four feet taller than he was. Next to him was a two-man bucksaw leaning against the tree stump where he had placed his foot to pose for the photo. His black hair was cut short and made his bushy mustache seem exaggerated on his youthful face.

I wondered if this young man had been a resident of the cabin that I was now standing in. I sat down and stretched back out, still holding the photo in my hands. I just needed to rest for a minute and get my bearings.

The sun was just coming back up on the east side of the horizon when I woke. I had slept half a day and an entire night away and really needed to urinate. It was an effort to sit my sore body up and painfully pull myself into the standing position as stiff as I was. My legs ached up into my hips and my back felt bruised and swollen. Not wanting to push too hard I tried to move slowly as the blood in my head pounded out a heartbeat rhythm that echoed painfully from ear to ear. The cool morning air felt comforting as I stepped outside the cabin and looked through my good eye for a shrub to pee in. Several feet away stood the perfect candidate for my much needed relief, so I stepped forward I began to pee.

Now, when a man pees, he does his most clear thinking, planning and reflecting. As I was "reflecting," I took in my surroundings with my good eye, noting how perfect the area was with its majestic mountain ranges, rugged rocks, thick dense trees… two adult male critters, one black and one red, staring at me not more than ten feet away!

I don't know why I felt embarrassed that they were watching me during my private moment. I couldn't finish fast enough and I wanted to be done quickly but my bladder simply needed more time to finish. Finally, I was able to regain my composure and salvage what was left of my dignity. My observers hadn't moved an inch. They just stood there, watching with their piercing little black eyes. Curious, I stood there and stared back at them but they just watched, emotionless and cold. I slowly turned away and returned back to the cabin. Once inside, I peered through the small openings of the window shutters but they were gone. Stepping back towards the door the larger male with the scar was standing just outside, as if waiting for me. Getting the idea he wanted me outdoors, I passed cautiously through the doorway and stepped out into the morning light towards him. He turned his body and started moving towards the glacier, not taking his eyes off of me. I was relieved he hadn't felt the need to lead me by my shoulder again.

As we approached the glacier, the air was much cooler against the massive ice. The sound of water trickling down the rocks broke the silence. Ahead I could see the red male, crouching down with his back to our approach. He was leaning over a cow elk on the ground beside the water pulling at the skin, exposing the meat and eating the raw flesh. The sight of him with blood on his giant hands and face made him look even more frightening than ever. As he bit into the meat, his white teeth were shining with crimson and displayed a set of pronounced and razor-sharp canine teeth.

My escort reached down and pulled at the front shoulder of the elk and ripped off a sizeable piece of meat and without looking, tossed it at my feet. At this point, they both went back to work at consuming their own meal. I stood there watching these two feed and couldn't bring myself to move until my lack of participation caught their attention. First the red male stopped and turned his beady eyes towards me, which made the other stop and turn his attention on me as well.

I felt pressured. The look on their faces was like that of two parents looking at a son who just climbed back in through a window at two in the morning. I felt like I was about to be scolded, so I reluctantly reached down and picked up the large piece of meat. Still they waited, not moving, looking at me with those hard black eyes. Surrendering to the idea, I sank my teeth into the raw meat, pulling away a bite and began to slowly chew the rubbery flesh.

Satisfied with my progress, they turned back towards their feast and resumed eating. I consumed enough to quiet my stomach and stepped forward to put the rest down. The two seemed unconcerned and ignored me as I stepped into the small pool of water running from the glacier and drank. The ice cold water felt good on my face and tasted cool and refreshing. Despite the events of the past twenty four hours I still enjoyed the clean, cold, pure mountain water.

Taking advantage of their attention on food, I headed back towards the cabin and saw the young male heading my way, accompanied by a small female. She was about four and a half feet tall and so skinny compared to the others that she looked fragile by comparison. She looked at me with intense curiosity as she positioned herself on the other side of the young male, peeking around his shoulder. Her nose was turned up and looked like a little hairy Shirley Temple with big wide curious eyes. In an ugly sort of way, she was absolutely cute.

As they approached, I stepped back and gave them a wide path to pass so as not to appear aggressive or upset the small female. Her little eyes never blinked, as her wide eyes studied every inch of me with curiosity and distrust. Expressionless, she spit out her tongue and blew air past it making the "Plbbbbt" I had heard coming from within the cave yesterday. I think it was her way of saying 'I don't like the looks of you.' This sound took me by surprise and I laughed out loud, again startling the young male and scaring the crap out of the little female. He put his hand on her back and pushed her along the trail as he picked up the pace to a trot. Quickly, I turned away and headed for the cabin again, hoping not to have upset the two youths too much.

Back at the cabin I inspected the wooden shutters and noticed they were fastened by several thick straps of leather. I pulled them open exposing the windows and allowing the mountain air to circulate inside the dark and musty cabin. The light coming in gave me a much better look at the inside of the rooms and its few contents. Sitting on the shelf was a lantern that had long ago rusted through, but the glass and wick were still intact. There were several empty cans and an old blue porcelain covered coffee pot that looked to be in good shape. Seeing there was no stove or fire place, I wondered how these guys kept warm or cooked for that matter? The most interesting find was tucked away in the corner of the shelf wrapped in a soft, oil-soaked leather wrap.

The nickel plated Colt .45 was once a beauty but now had a fair amount of rust and tarnish. It was an old revolver that still advanced the cylinder when the hammer was drawn back. It had been put away empty and deliberately wrapped with oil in hopes of preserving the metal and keeping it fully functional. It seemed odd that it had been put away separate from the bullets; did the previous owner not need any kind of protection? This was wild country with many dangers. What good was an unloaded weapon out here in the sticks? I took my time cleaning it up as much as I could with the oily wrap and then put it away.

My next objective was to have a closer look at the bullets that I had found the previous night. I retrieved the small pouch containing the bullets and the photo from the support beam above my bed and removed the contents for another inspection. The bullets were old and green with corrosion but three of the five looked to be in good useable shape. The corner of the old wool blanket seemed to do an adequate job of cleaning the three bullets and getting the majority of the corrosion from the brass. I took a closer look at the photo, hoping to find some sort of answer in the young logger's face and his surroundings. I wondered how this photo had found its way here, in the middle of these woods, in this cabin, and who had taken the time to build it? I put the three good bullets and two questionable rounds back into the small pouch and hung it back on the beam. I began my "spring cleaning" and gathered up items that needed disposing.

I was interrupted by a large shadow passing in front of the window and looked up to see 'Red' standing just outside of the cabin, impatiently waiting for me to come out. I placed the picture under the blanket, stood up, and made my exit into the sunlight towards my giant companion. As I approached, my escort had already turned and started making his way towards the opening of the cave. Following Red, I was impressed by the sheer size of this male. His huge calves made any bodybuilder look as if they were mere amateurs. The solid mass that erupted from his hips and blew outward into thick dense shoulders looked as if they could actually carry the weight of the world upon them. In all of my travels, I have not seen a sculpture or statue ever depict such a magnificent specimen. I saw 'Radar', the big eared youngster, nervously pacing back and forth at the entrance of the cave. He looked anxious about something. Red stopped at the mouth of the cave, turned and faced me, his dark small black mean eyes showing no emotion. After a short pause that felt like an eternity, he stepped backwards and gestured for me to go inside ahead of him.

Looking into the dark opening of the cave and not knowing what was on the other side gave me that sick feeling again. The overpowering smell of sweat, rot, and vomit was heavy in the moist air and was coming from somewhere within the opening. I knew running was not an option so I took a deep breath of clean air, lowered my head and stepped into the pungent darkness. After a few moments, my eyes became accustomed to the dark interior. I could see sunlight coming through a small opening about twenty yards farther in from where I was standing. The smell and thick rancid air was overwhelming and the urge to vomit was getting stronger, but somehow I managed to keep the raw meat in my stomach where it was for now. I was able to make out several shapes in the open area that were large rocks and several areas of grass and small twigs which appeared to be beds or sleeping areas on the ground for the residents. The room opened up into a large area with roughly a fifteen foot space between the solid smooth rock ceiling and the hard dirt floor. I was surprised to see the cave split off to the right and appeared to go much deeper and out of sight. The sound of water flowing some-where in the distance was comforting and constant. It sounded like a small stream and gave promise of a supply of water. Off to my left was the figure of what appeared to be another one of the tribe members. This one was uneasy and making an effort not to be seen by maintaining a low position near the wall, never taking his gaze off of me.

As I stood there wondering how many members actually lived here, the silence was broken by the sound of the shy little 'Raspberry' as she let out an odd sounding burst of noise from directly behind, scaring the crap out of me. I jumped half out of my boots and instinctively moved quickly to the side. My startled action set off her reaction, with a terrifying scream which echoed down the walls of the cave and seemed to continue on forever. A pair of huge, foul smelling hands grabbed me and I was effortlessly thrust to the hard dirt floor. Still very sore from the rough play with Scarface, I hit the ground hard with my own surprised scream. Without moving I waited as the sounds of someone or something came over from behind me. This made me uneasy as the footsteps stopped just out of my view. A large and gentle hand took my elbow and pulled me carefully upwards helping me to my feet. I warily and slowly turned to see an almost pure white male with wrinkles all around his tired eyes and sloped shoulders, like that of an old man. His eyes were kind and wise, but also showed the strength and power to command respect. He was a good foot and a half taller than I was and looked down at me with the most brilliant blue eyes I had ever seen. These eyes possessed a calm, quiet stare that made me feel surprisingly at ease. Even though he was elderly and the signs of arthritis were present, this male was thick and well muscled with oversized forearms like the cartoon Popeye. I will respectfully refer to him as Elder.

The light coming in through the entrance was suddenly blocked off by the massive form of Scarface coming inside with a large portion of fresh meat in his giant hands. He stopped abruptly and looked at me with an obvious irritation and disapproval, as if he did not want me inside the cave. With his piercing stare and giant presence, I became very uncomfortable as he approached without taking his eyes off of me. He came almost directly in front of me before brushing by and continued further into the opening to the right of the entrance and disappeared deep into the cave and out of sight. The elderly male then turned me around and gestured for me to follow Scarface but kept his giant hand on my shoulder as we moved deeper into the opening to the right. It became so dark that I couldn't see my hand in front of my face but the huge hand on my shoulder kept me moving at a steady pace into the darkness. At one point, I stumbled on something hard on the ground and almost tripped but the hand on my shoulder prevented my fall as his other hand grabbed my elbow. He kept me supported and steady, guiding me forward with a gentle but solid pressure.

We continued on for about ten minutes into the darkness when I noticed silhouettes of the walls ahead and some light from somewhere far ahead. The sound of water was so close I could feel the cool dampness in the air and was caught off guard when my legs were suddenly calf deep in cold flowing water. The water was a small stream in the darkness that felt to be two paces wide and running from right to left at a smooth flow. The light ahead became brighter as we continued past the stream, and I was able to see more of my surroundings in the cave. We had been walking on fairly level ground but now we were moving up a slight incline towards the light. The distant illumination had given enough light to see that this cave was much larger now with ceilings as high as twenty feet and a good twenty feet from side to side. I could see in the distance, blue skies and brilliant sunlight with vines and plant growth covering most of the opening of another cave entrance. It felt as if we had just walked through a tunnel from one side of the mountain top to the other.

We continued into a large area with the opening directly in front of us. The entrance was about six feet high by fifteen feet wide that ended with small points at both sides. The mouth of the cave looked like the opening of an eye with green overgrowth for eyelashes.

As I stood in the large open area about ten feet from the entrance, there were two more openings that went back into the mountain to my left and one more to my right as I faced the light. I was aware of several other tribe members peering from deeper within the cave. They kept just enough distance that I couldn't see exactly how many there were. The hand on my shoulder let go and the Elder ambled past me to the entrance and held the vines aside and looked back at me, as if to invite me out. Thinking that we were going to leave this nasty smelling room, I approached his position but was stopped suddenly short when he placed his hand on my chest. Surprised, I took my eyes off of him and looked outside beyond the edge to see nothing but open space.

Inhaling the cool clean air, I looked down and was shocked to see the ground six hundred feet below. From where I stood I could see several distant mountain ranges that looked unfamiliar and very far away. We were in the center of a sheer rock cliff that provided absolutely no entry or escape from this particular opening. This meant that an escape from this point would be impossible without a parachute. The view was breathtaking and the ranges seemed to go on forever as I watched a hawk patrolling the skies for food far below. I stepped back into the cave and waited for my eyes to adjust to the darkness again. If someone wanted to hide in the mountains and never be seen again, this was truly the place to be.

Glancing around I looked into one of the openings and noticed several occupants peering back at me with mild curiosity, but what caught my eye was a long piece of rope that lay coiled on the floor. Elder looked down at the rope and then back at me with an 'I know what you're thinking,' kind of look that told me anything I had going on in my head about that rope had better be left alone.

Elder placed his hands on my shoulders and positioned himself behind me, holding firm but not to the point of any discomfort. With a low tone, the voice of the old giant behind me barked out three quick commands that echoed throughout the entire cavern. The volume sent shivers down my spine and cut through the air with an eerie sound. It was the combination of a woman's scream, the lungs of an elk and the bawl of a bear. In human words, I'd interpret it as, "Now!" What happened next was frightening and fascinating. I felt like the circus freak with everyone coming out to take a look.

I was standing in the middle of a large room with the cave opening to my back and a giant with his huge hands on my shoulders. I watched in amazement as members appeared from the three inner-cave openings and walked around us. They studied me intently as if to decide who I was and wondered what I was doing in their home. It was difficult to keep track of how many there were, but I'm certain I saw at least twenty-five as they all came in a crowd and left just as quickly as they had arrived. The intense smell combined with the excitement was almost too much for me, and I caught myself gagging, trying hard not to vomit. My stomach started to react to the raw meat breakfast in my belly mixed with the pungent odor that filled my nose. The creatures were all sizes and varied colors as they passed by for their curious inspection of the outsider. I too looked back with amazement and awe as their sheer size was intimidating and frightening. Several smaller members peered from a distance with curiosity, but stayed off to the side. One extended his hand out to touch my shirt only to be hissed away by a large, mean, older looking female.

The female stepped right in front of me and looked down her nose at me with a glare that would stop the most hardened criminal in his tracks. She was heavily muscled with scattered gray hair showing up throughout her entire body and looked like a linebacker with an attitude. Her breath had that nasty smell as if she had been eating rotting flesh and been sick from it. As she towered above me, everyone in the room seemed to pause to see what she would do as she stared at me with her mean, fearless, tired eyes. Without a sound, she began to bare her teeth, which were surprisingly white, and made a low hissing sound. Elder, still standing behind me, stopped her with a sharp tone. Knowing she'd been corrected, 'Grumpy' turned quickly away and left the area, visibly agitated.

I noticed everyone shared the features of high cheekbones and a somewhat wide lower jawbone, with that proud Native American look. Not one single member looked fragile or weak in any way. In fact, despite their hygiene they were the most amazing creatures I had ever come in contact with on the planet. I saw there were an equal number of females as there were males in my quick survey. The females certainly didn't come across weak or less capable than the males. Their movements, appearance and behavior were very upright and human with the same individualism as everyday people. These creatures had their own characteristics, looks and features that set them apart, very much like the human race.

Suddenly, as quickly as they had appeared, the room was empty again except for me and the Elder, but the heavy stench lingered long after the guests were gone. Scarface had also come in and disappeared with the rest of the members. On the way back, Elder placed his reassuring hand on my shoulder as we made our way past the water to the opening on the rockslide. Once again out in the open, I hungrily sucked in the fresh mountain air. Radar patiently waiting to escort me back to my perspective residence. Back at the cabin, I had a new and profound appreciation for the smell of clean fresh air and took it in with a renewed enthusiasm. I never realized how much I enjoyed the pure nature air as much as I did right now and the cabin was a welcome relief.

I sat on the edge of the bed and looked around at my small surroundings and noticed someone had carved the words, "The only way out is in" above the door. I'm not too sure how I felt about the hand carved phrase, but I knew whoever wrote those words was long gone from here. I wondered what had become of the previous resident and who or what brought him all way out here in the first place? Was the prior owner of this cabin brought here like me or had he chosen to live here with these foul smelling neighbors?

Throughout the next week we seemed to get into a routine of eating the raw meat from the elk carcass by the glacier and leaving me to my own devices within the walls of the cabin and the limited range of real estate outside. My eye and lip healed up nicely and the stiffness in my body diminished. I began to feel almost back to normal and was losing a little bit of weight from my new diet of raw meat and greens.

I don't know why we do it, but looking down at the elk meat, I started thinking about my mother's home cooking; chicken dinner, lasagna, burgers and other items not found on the menu out here in the mountains. The thought of sitting down at the table with her and my father and eating a home cooked meal seemed like a far away dream and made my stomach growl. The only way I would enjoy a home cooked meal was to find a way to leave this place. I looked around and the thought seemed impossible at the moment. There was always a tribe member around close, keeping a diligent eye on my every move.

Sunday Morning Visitor

There was a firm knock at the door. Without looking up from his morning paper, Victor said to his wife, "Look honey, Ed McMann is here with our sweepstakes check." Keeping up with his dry humor she replied quickly, "No, it's the pool boy, he always comes on Sunday after you leave the house."

With a quick grin she turned away from the kitchen with her mid-length silver hair flowing over her oversized red flannel shirt and headed towards the front door drying her hands on a kitchen towel. Half way to the entrance she saw there was a uniformed police officer at the door and her pleasant smile faded quickly. He appeared to be in his mid forties with silver-flecked, black hair and a small manicured goatee on his otherwise boyish face. Standing just over six feet tall he was lean and had that cowboy look, including deep creases in his brow line to reflect troubled times, which could be the reason for his visit today. Quietly she hesitated and said, "There is a police officer at the front door Vic."

Hearing her serious tone he knew this wasn't one of their playful sparring matches and quietly set his paper to the side. He rose from his chair and followed her to the door with curiosity and concern showing in his tired face. Victor had seen his own share of troubled times through his years but had always forged through the bitter times with hard work, determination and sweat. Just less than six feet tall he was thick through the shoulders and had leather skin and square jaw that gave him a no-nonsense look. Yet, with genuine kindness in his eyes and a quick-to-smile pleasantness, his demeanor was mostly about hard work and having something to show at each day's end.

"Are you Victor and Sandra Walker?" asked the officer politely.

"Yes indeed, what can we do for you?" said Victor in an uneasy tone.

"Well sir, my name is Officer Tim Hutchins from Ravalli county Sheriff's Department, and I've just come in from the Bitterroot Valley area. Do you have a son named Turley Eugene Walker?"

"Yes, that's our son, is he alright?" Sandra asked quickly.

"Right now, I couldn't say Mrs. Walker, but I have a few questions that I hope you can help me clear up. I certainly don't mean to cause any worry for the two of you, but the forest service office was notified two days ago by some hikers that found your son's camp.

And from the looks of things up there, we have reason to believe that your son may be in trouble."

"What kind of trouble, did he fall from the cliffs?" Victor questioned.

"No sir, not that we can find, but his camp was left in a bit of a mess and all his belongings were abandoned. When did you last speak to him Mr. Walker?" the officer asked.

"Well," Victor replied, "He called me about a week ago and said he was going up to the top of Kootenai Mountain to hike around the upper summit where he spent most of his time as a child. I've got a Forest Service map of that area; do you think you can point out where his camp is?"

"Yes sir. I spent an entire day up on top and had a good look at the camp and the surrounding area, I also have some of his personal effects that were left behind and several photos to show the layout at the camp if you won't mind looking them over," said the officer.

"I'm sorry Officer Hutchins. I don't mean to keep you out on the porch. Please come inside," Vic replied.

Respectfully, the officer removed his hat and after wiping his feet, stepped into the home anxiously clutching a large manila envelope in his hands.

"From what I could tell, he had set up camp close to a nice big pine just beyond the summit and a short distance down the northwest side. The sleeping bag was never completely set out and the camp gear was mostly untouched, except for what the squirrels chewed through."

"Was this a nice little flat spot just below a small rock slide area? It would almost be in the upper most point facing the Bitterroot-Selway Wilderness area," Victor inquired.

"Yes, as a matter of fact that's precisely where it was, you must have spent a fair share of time up there to know that," the officer answered with surprise, "I have the pictures right here if you would like to have a look at the site."

As Victor leaned in for a closer look at the photos, he wasn't at all surprised that it was the same camp location they had used a few times over the years. Even looking at the photos he could tell from the scene there had been a struggle. The picture showed disturbed ground where the pine needles were strewn about and several signs of some deep gouges in the ground where the dirt below had been unearthed by several inches.

"Sir, there are several things that don't add up in that area. We found his loaded pistol and one shell casing indicating only one single shot had been fired. There was also a fair amount of blood at the base of that tree as you can see from the third photo." The officer stated, looking nervously up at Sandra.

Seeing his concern she spoke calm and steady, flashing a small rehearsed smile and replied, "Our son has been in the military for many years, Officer Hutchins. I've had a lot of time to prepare myself for who might come knocking on that door. Unless you have come here with his recovered body, I refuse to believe that Kootenai Mountain has taken my boy. He's a fighter like his father, and until he is found you can be assured Turley won't give up easily."

"What kind of tracks are we looking at here Officer; grizzly, wolf or mountain lion?" Victor asked speculatively.

"Well sir, that's where I have the most difficulty with this situation because there were no tracks. None of us could find any tracks in or out other than your son's. It's the oddest thing," Officer Hutchins stated.

"There has to be tracks, nothing walks that mountain or makes that kind of mess without leaving some kind of tracks," Victor responded.

"You see, sir, there were four of us up on that mountain top, looking carefully for some kind of clue as to what your son encountered below that slide. We all came up with absolutely nothing, even up to a half mile of circular coverage," Officer Hutchins answered.

"Sandra, call Jeff and see what he is doing for the next couple of days. Looks like we're going to have to show these uniform boys how to find a track in the woods," Victor said with a light hearted smile. "In my experience nothing ever climbs on that mountain without leaving some kind of track behind Officer Hutchins, you just have to know what you're looking for. Is there anything else that might have caught your attention?"

"I have all of his effects in my truck from the campsite, which will give you a chance to see what he might still have with him." Looking down at the photos on the table, Officer Hutchins continued, "From the pictures you can see that there was a fair amount of blood here at the base of the tree. When I dug into the dirt, the amount of blood left behind was about six or seven inches deep. That tells me that whatever left that much blood had to have sat stationary for quite a spell or was bleeding fast to lose all that fluid."

"The pistol was a good ten feet to the left of the tree, but the single shell casing was right here by the base. It looks as if there was some pretty deep digs into the soil out in front of the tree and up against the blood area. The deep marks are big enough that something heavy was pushed or pulled through this space and indicate signs of a serious struggle. I was unable to find any kind of animal or boot track in the entire area other than those I believe to be your sons. Sir, I have been called on to investigate many cases in the National Forest and this is the first time I've had nothing for tracks or evidence. I grew up in the Bitterroot valley and have spent my entire childhood in the Bitterroot Mountain Range. Like you, I believe that nothing passes through the woods without leaving its mark, that's why this case is so peculiar."

"I appreciate your straight forward talk and don't place any doubt on your abilities

Officer Hutchins, but you understand that I'm one of those men that has to see it for myself. I know that mountain range also, and it's always been full of mystery and surprises. Were your men able to find any blood or trace of anything within your half mile range for an indication of direction?" Victor asked.

"Not one single drop, and nothing to show that anything of size passed by, and of course the rock slide above it is too steep and rough for bear or mountain lion to pass, especially if it had anything to carry or drag." Hutchins replied. "Even so, one of our men combed it pretty carefully anyway hoping to find something that we could use."

"I will come out to the truck with you to get his things. Maybe a different set of eyes on that mountain top will reveal some signs of what took place," Victor said solemnly.

Officer Hutchins turned with a polite nod to Sandra and headed for the front door clutching his hat. Once outside he placed his hat on his head and turned to Victor, "His pistol is exactly as I found it, with the exception that the hammer was still cocked and there was a live round still in the chamber. Sir, with your son being a military man, I tend to believe that something went seriously wrong for him to shoot once and be stripped of his weapon. I apologize that this kind of news is the only reason that you and I have met. Here is my card and if you don't mind keeping me up to date on your findings." Extending his right hand he shook Victors hand firmly. "I live in Stevensville, right off the highway and will be available to assist in any way I can."

Victor stood beside a medium sized cardboard box and watched as Officer Hutchins backed down his driveway. He always hoped it would never end like this—a visit from a polite uniformed man and watching him leave, providing him with the last known possessions of his son. His gut feeling told him a different story was happening here. His son was out there, alive and needed his father's help to get back home. Choking back his emotion, he bent down and took the box into the house where Sandra was clearing the table.

"Did you get hold of Jeff?" He inquired.

"Yes, he will be here this evening in time for supper." She replied.

Trying to smile through the seriousness he teased, "If it wasn't for your cooking, he wouldn't come until long after the dinner hour."

Reaching out she grabbed his hand and looking him in the eye she said with a trembling tone, "Victor, you go bring our son back home to me."

"You know I'm way too stubborn to come back empty handed honey, that's why you married me," Victor responded.

Welcome Guest

The tired horseman sat on the front porch of his large log home, the sounds of chicken frying on the stove could be heard somewhere inside the kitchen. Every now and then he could hear a pan hitting against the stove or the water would turn on and off in the big stainless steel sink. Vic sat still, deep in thought as he watched for his best friend Jeff to arrive. The wait paid off as far in the distance he could see an old rusty blue 1965 Ford truck coming off the county road and turning onto his long, winding, dusty driveway. "He's here," Vic announced over his shoulder, not taking his eyes off the truck in the distance. He watched in quiet amusement as the truck blew a cloud of blue smoke from its tail pipe and traveled down the lane leaving a trail of dust behind.

Jeff was never interested in fancy clothes, trucks, houses or anything that would make him indebted to a bank. He'd had that old Ford truck as long as anyone could remember, but he was always content with his life, which balances out to happy. As he pulled into the driveway he pulled up beside Vic's new Dodge pickup with a low belching backfire. Jeff opened the loud squeaky Ford door and with a broad smile said, "You still driving that old piece of crap Vic?"

"I'm afraid so, Jeff. Can't seem to keep my Ford running long enough to get any use out of it, so I settled for the Dodge," he shot back with a smile.

"Holy smokes," Jeff blurted out, "Is she making her famous fried chicken? I swear I can smell it from here!"

"I never get fried chicken when it's just the two of us. You know she only makes it when you come around Jeff. It's your reward for getting me out from under her feet for a while. Even better, she's making extra so we can take some with us," Vic answered.

As he crossed the driveway he carried with him a large backpack that looked over-stuffed with some old school wooden snow shoes firmly secured to the back of it. As Vic watched him come up the three steps onto the porch he realized how good it was to see Jeff again and how rare a friendship like theirs was. Standing up, Vic embraced his friend with a hug and with a hearty pat on the back he stepped back and pulled the front door open for his guest. "I know you're only here for the fine dining," Vic teased, smiling at his friend.

"Boy, you sure know a way to a man's heart, Sandra!" Jeff said as he strode in behind her and gave her a quick one armed shoulder hug and peck on the cheek.

Looking up from her stove a warm friendly smile came across her face, "So glad you could make it Jeff," she said sincerely.

"I can't send the old man into the woods all alone on such an adventure as this. Somebody needs to keep an eye on him anyway," Jeff responded.

"Get comfortable in the guest room. Dinner will be ready to eat in about ten minutes," Sandra said.

"Is my timing good or what?" Jeff asked Vic smiling. "Let's have a look at that map and see what we know so far."

Looking over the map, Jeff and Vic talked in low tones about the details Officer Hutchins had covered and what they both knew about the rugged mountain. After dinner the two went out on the porch to go over their plans for the next several days and tried to mentally map out how to cover the distances that might have been overlooked by the others. Jeff was quiet and serious when it was mentioned there were no tracks and the others came up empty handed.

Scanning the pictures, he mentioned that there was a similar incident not too many years back of a missing hiker up in Canada where no tracks of any kind could be found. Jeff and Vic both agreed that there had to be something overlooked by the others that would give them clues as to what took place on that mountain. All walks of life leave some kind of trace behind, it's just a matter of recognizing what it is. Jeff was one of the best trackers out there and Vic was grateful to have him on this particular hunt. After two hours of planning and going over details of the photos, the two decided to turn in for the night. The next morning they would be leaving Vic's house at 3:30 a.m.

At 3:00 a.m., Jeff and Vic woke to the smell of fresh coffee and the sound of bacon sizzling on the stove. Sandra had gotten up early to make sure they left the house with a proper breakfast and a good cup of coffee instead of the truck stop brew in Missoula.

"Thanks again for the hospitality Sandra. Sorry you had to get up so early for us," Jeff said politely.

"Don't you worry about me, I'm going right back to my warm bed for a few more hours of sleep. Don't you let anything happen to him," She said nodding towards Vic, who was gulping down the last of his coffee and bacon.

"I heard that," Vic said moving in towards his wife. With a quick kiss on the lips he finished, "Bye Sweetie, I'll call you in a couple of days."

They rode towards Missoula reminiscing about old hunts and past adventures they had shared. They took greatest pleasure in some of the tough spots they had somehow lived through over the years. Once they got through Lolo and into Florence the conversation became more serious, and Jeff finally asked his good friend, "Vic, I know we have been through the toughest storms and faced some hard choices in the past, but you need to be prepared for what could be the worst case scenario. Are you going to be able to handle this if it becomes a recovery mission instead of a rescue?"

Taking his eyes off the road for a second Vic looked at his best friend and replied, "I am ready for whatever might be in front of us Jeff, and you know that. I have thought it over quite a bit and here is what I believe. You and I both know that Turley is no stranger to tough times and hard choices. He's faced them whether from spending so much time here in these mountains with the two of us or the time spent fighting on foreign soil. If he is dead, I think it's only right for you and me to find him and be the ones to bring my son home. At least this way he passed on U.S. soil and in the greatest mountain range on earth rather than at the hands of an enemy in a combat zone. From what I know of my boy, he would never give up or go down easy without giving the fight of his life. Yes, I am ready for the worst, but I feel in my gut that he is still alive and out there somewhere. Until otherwise proven, I am going to bet on my faith in his ability to stay alive."

Just short of Stevensville, they turned right off of Highway 93 towards Kootenai Mountain and parked at the familiar trailhead. After checking for loose items on their packs, they both donned their gear and each checked the other's load for final inspection. With the rushing sound of the creek below, they both paused to look up the steep trail. This was the first time they had come up here with such a mindset. This was not for the hunt, for the adventure or for mindless thrill seeking. What lie ahead may be heartbreak and give them answers they didn't want. Today was truly different.

Jeff rested his hand on Vic's shoulder as they stood in silence at the trailhead, the light breeze rustling his salt and pepper hair. Today he looked serious, tired, and heavy in thought but he was more than ready for the challenges that lie ahead. "Let's go get your boy," he said quietly as he stepped forward and headed up the familiar trail.

From Above

There was an odd sense of tense excitement in the air, and restlessness within the tribe was apparent. I watched the members come and go in small groups and leave for hours at a time, returning with bear grass, small tree branches, and skins from rabbits and other smaller animals. It appeared they were gathering supplies for the cold winter months ahead. Red's behavior made it clear that I was not to leave the immediate area and to leave the wood and other plant life in the area undisturbed. His eyes drilled through me as he stood uncomfortably close and gestured for me to move back in the direction of the cabin.

Now I felt like a captive with limited privileges and only enough room to move around, as long as it was in full view of the five acre area. My range allowed me to get water from the glacier runoff and meat from the elk that was cooling by the icy water. The green leaves I could eat seemed to be running low and it was becoming more difficult to find edible portions of meat.

It was a cold and chilly morning with frost all over the ground, but the clear blue sky showed hope that the day would be warming up to a reasonable temperature. I had just walked out to my favorite brush pile for my early morning tinkle, when I noticed that only a few of the tribe were in sight and they were briskly walking towards the opening of the cave. It looked odd that everyone was heading for the cave and leaving me unattended, but I had other things in hand. As I finished my own personal business, I went back around to the side of the cabin to check on my clothes that I had left to dry the night before and found them still fairly damp but was willing to wear them anyway.

Once in my semi-dry clothes, I strolled out into the open and see if any of the tribe members were in sight and found no one around at all. Odd, I couldn't recall any time that at least one of the tribe members wasn't looming in the shadows to keep me in their sight. Then I heard a sound that I hadn't heard since I had been brought up on this mountain. It was the engine of a small plane! It was down in the valley below our site and most likely an outfitter looking over the area to choose a good hunting spot for this year's elk hunt. I noticed it was getting closer to our location and would probably fly right over our area. Out of curiosity I waited to see where it would go and saw in the distance as it approached the slide area. It was still about a mile away when it passed our location and glided by without any signs that its occupants saw me. All at once, I heard a blowing sound of an adult tribe member off to my right and knew in an instant that my actions had been the wrong choice.

I glanced up to see Scarface standing there looking at me with anger, disappointment, and fear in his face. His look was all I needed. I immediately cast my eyes down at the ground realizing I had just put the tribe in jeopardy of being discovered and lowered my shoulders to show my own shame and remorse. He turned away without a sound and walked back to the opening of the cave, never looking back. I too retreated back to my cabin with regret. Of course they didn't want to be found! How thoughtless I had been to put them at risk. What I had grown up with and gotten used to, was a completely different culture than what these mysterious creatures were used to. The sight of an airplane was common in my world but to this tribe it meant deadly exposure. My lack of awareness could have put curious people right here at this location and jeopardized the long kept secret this tribe counts on for its very survival. I vowed to myself on this day I would never again put this species in danger. I never want to be responsible for providing proof to the hungry, intrusive media that the legendary Bigfoot actually does exist.

The Hunt

With meat supplies running low, I knew
they would soon be looking for replacement
food and anticipated some kind of hunt in
the near future. I had grown used to the idea
that my stay here was going to be extended
for a while as I was falling into the routine
of their habits and their lives. I found
myself looking at them as more human than
primates, and the differences between our
two species was becoming less noticeable. I
watched as Red and Scarface, with Radar on
their heels, approached the cabin from the

glacier carrying what appeared to be large sections of elk antlers in their hands. The antlers were huge to me but looked small in the hands of these hunters. Without slowing down, they passed by and Radar dropped a piece of antler at my feet and kept his eyes on me until I bent down to pick it up. It looked like today was going to be different. All three looked as if they expected me to accompany them into the woods with my prehistoric tool.

Making our way across the rocks of the slide, the three seemed impatient with me as I moved much slower than they did through the treacherous footing. After we passed the slide, the pace quickened to the point that I almost had to jog to keep up with the hunting party. Didn't they realize that my legs were much shorter, and I was not conditioned like they were? Throughout the past couple of nights, I had heard the sounds of the elk bugling in the distance as the bulls challenged one another, looking for a good fight. Something told me we were in pursuit of that particular food source to store up for the coming winter months. I had grown accustomed to eating raw meat and nibbling on the green leaves of the underbrush and seemed to be tolerating it pretty well.

The trees and undergrowth were thick and difficult for me to navigate with the pace they had set, but I did my best to stay with them and maintain quiet movement. It seemed as if we had only gone a couple of miles when Scarface stopped suddenly, turned around and lunged straight towards me with a wild look in his eyes. Behind him I saw Red and Radar move in separate directions off the trail and vanish from view. Scarface rushed towards me with his eyes locked on mine. I stood still, unsure and uneasy about what was coming. Scarface rushed past with ferocious speed, circling his arm around my waist and pulling me into the brush, knocking the wind from my lungs. With a quick, powerful movement he hoisted my body onto his broad shoulders and positioned my arms around his thick neck as we moved towards a large pine tree about fifty yards away. When we approached the tree, his body tensed up and he sprung upwards towards the lower branches of the tall solid tree. With grace and power he quickly pulled us both up into the tree until we were twenty feet from the ground.

At this point, he repositioned me with my chest into the trunk of the tree and his body behind me, with his arms around my body and the tree, he held me firm and still. It happened so quickly that I had little time to react. I stayed still, pinned to the tree by the huge smelly beast behind me, clutching my elk antler in amazement. Behind me I could feel his heart beat against my back and smell his hot rancid breath on my face. I knew that I physically couldn't move and the thought of making noise was probably not a good idea. Slowly, he released his right arm from around me and held out his own elk antler about six inches from the tree and struck the tree with three quick thumps and waited.

In the distance uphill from our position, I heard the same three short thumps on a tree, followed by three more thumps further away to our left. It dawned on me they were communicating their positions with the sounds of their antlers on the trees. I was fascinated by their way of communication but found it confusing that we were positioned twenty feet up a tree, until I heard a distinct and familiar sound—something I hadn't heard in many days. It was the unmistakable voices of fellow humans—a female talking to a male—possibly two hikers moving along the trail in the distance. I could not hear what was said but it was no doubt the sound of people engaged in conversation. I wondered why these beasts were not at all interested in this unsuspecting couple, and why I had been chosen to be pulled into their world. I felt both excited and sad to hear the voices, as if the prospect of having a conversation with someone in the future seemed a bit unsure in my current state of captivity. We stayed in the tree for roughly thirty minutes after the voices had long faded away.

Once again I heard two thumps of an antler on the base of a tree somewhere to the far left of our position. This sound was a familiar one, always in the woods, always the same. I had dismissed this sound in the past as trees knocking into one another in the breeze. I now wonder how many times throughout my years in the woods I heard the sounds of trees when actually it was knocking or communication between these fascinating creatures. Scarface returned the call by striking the tree with two short thumps. He relaxed his firm grip allowing air into my aching lungs and maneuvered me down to the soft earth below. When he let me go, I fell forward as my legs had gone numb, but he caught my fall and steadied me up against the tree, in his not so gentle way. I held on to the tree for a minute to regain my bearings but my escort was ready to leave. With Scarface leading the way, we headed back to the trail where Radar and Red were already waiting. They both looked restless and anxious, turning away quickly as we approached and proceeded back down the trail we had occupied earlier. With Red in the lead and Radar following close behind, Scarface motioned for me to follow as he came in behind me, antler in hand, and the swift pace continued.

After an hour of quick-paced travel, we stepped off the game trail and moved into a small cool basin with dense growth and much thicker trees. I couldn't help but notice that I was the only one making any noise on the ground and that the pace had slowed down considerably. I became more conscious of my foot placement and moved through the trees with stealth and silence. We continued quietly for another fifteen minutes until the silence was interrupted as Red lunged into the thick undergrowth, disappearing over the hill with Radar close behind. All around me, I heard the sounds of an elk herd blowing and running through the woods, trying to put distance from where we had discovered them and the hungry hunters that pursued. Scarface stood still, listening; his head tilted back smelling the air and looking uphill in the direction the other two had gone.

As quickly as the commotion began, it stopped and all went quiet. My beating heart was the loudest thing in the forest until I heard two thumps from an antler on a tree, not more than fifty yards away. Scarface brushed past me, and I followed close behind as we came to where the sound originated. Standing next to a small pine tree was Radar, towering over a large cow elk that he had brought down with his hunting tool which was ironically, an antler from another elk. Red was close by with a smaller yearling calf that he was already pulling through the underbrush towards Radar's position. Just beyond Radar, I saw some movement in the brush and watched in amazement as several other members of the tribe emerged from the trees pulling their bounty with them. This entire time I thought only the four of us were in this hunt. It came as no surprise that the others were able to follow along without me knowing. Not wasting any time, several other members emerged into view and began lifting the elk in pairs of two, carrying them back towards the rockslide several miles away.

Even Grumpy stepped out of the brush and wrapped her strong arms around the neck of one of the elk, shouldering her half of the incredible load along with another large female. Both made their way out to the trail. I counted seven elk being carried away and was amazed at the eerie silence of the entire event. Red pulled on the sleeve of my shirt and turned away from the elk and other members and the four of us continued down the trail away from their camp and slide area. Radar and Scarface were ahead of us by about a hundred yards, and Red was closing the distance with his long stride. We hadn't gone more than a mile when I heard a howl that sounded like a wolf in trouble.

The sound stopped everyone dead in their tracks and I practically slammed into the back of Red. Scarface looked concerned, Radar looked confused, and Red looked almost agitated by the sound. Turning around, we headed back down the trail we had just traveled. With Scarface leading the way, we moved fairly fast and were back in the brush where we had left the others and their elk not more than a half hour earlier. Quietly, Red held out his antler and knocked on the tree next to him with two methodical thumps. The immediate returning knocks were off to our right about a half mile away. Quickly, Scarface stepped away and with a masterful stride headed into the brush without a sound. Doing my best to keep pace and keep quiet, I stepped in behind Radar with Red at my heels. As we arrived to the area where the knocks had come from, I could hear something big in the brush with sounds of loud, labored breathing. Looking around I was conscious of several of the other members standing by quietly, half hidden in the thick brush.

Next to a small sapling was a nice large bull elk that had been taken down by one of the members. Only this time, the bull hadn't given up without a fight of his own and had seriously gored a sizable male member of the tribe. The labored breathing was coming from him as his stomach, just below the ribcage, was torn open exposing a couple ribs protruding from under his dark hairy hide. Below were some of his lower intestines protruding from a second open hole that was bleeding volumes of blood out into the soil beneath him.

Scarface gave a worried look over his shoulder at Red who pushed roughly past me to kneel down beside the large wounded male. Scarface stepped backwards a couple of steps and gently extended his arm to my chest and moved me back a few steps. I watched with intense curiosity as Red bowed his head low and placed his hands on the male's chest and shoulder. There was clearly a close connection between this male and Red as he began to rock back and forth, breathing the same labored rhythm as the injured male. Red stared into the eyes of the young male and looked just as wounded as the gored, bleeding hunter.

This was the first time I had ever seen so much emotion among any of the members, especially the stone cold Red. The younger male put his hands on Reds wrists and gripped in agony from his pain. He tried to sit up, bringing more pain and a fresh surge of blood from the wound in his lower stomach. No one moved or made a sound. Everyone was physically present but were silent leaving the two alone and isolated to share these last moments together.

There was no way the young male was going to leave here on his own, and the loss of blood was making him weaker with each breath. He knew he was dying and with his grip on Red, I'm convinced Red knew it too. Red knelt in closer, settled in on his right hip, and laid his head on the chest of the young male, wrapping his left arm over the younger male's neck. I watched in amazement as tears flowed from the eyes of the fierce Red, and quiet sobs echoed past his lips. Shamelessly, Red held tight to the young male and wept as the young one's last breaths faded to silence. With the breath gone, Red's mournful sobs became pronounced and rhythmic.

Even now, the members around us held fast like statues. Nothing moved in those woods except a fierce giant, brought to his knees by the passing of someone close, someone important and someone he loved.

After roughly ten more minutes, Red raised his head from the chest of the young male. He stood up and reached down to lift the deceased male to his own broad shoulders. With tears still escaping from his eyes, Red turned towards the elk and gazed at it for a moment as a sound came from deep within his chest. His head faced the skies and he let out a shrill howl that echoed throughout the lower valley and the elevated canyons above. It was the sound of pain, agony, and a profound ache from the heart of the creature making it. We all turned our backs on the area and left single file back towards the rock slide home, behind Red who walked ahead carrying the deceased. Quietly we left and no one touched or acknowledged the dead bull elk. It was left where it lay to rot in the open air and feed the scavengers that would come for it.

Rock Slide

Red carried the young male on his shoulders the entire distance back to the slide area as we all moved in silence. It was sobering to see the way the other members reacted to the death of the young male, especially the raw emotion Red had displayed. There was some close connection between the two and the impact on Red was clearly a difficult burden. We all moved single file throughout the distance, and not a single sound was uttered as I fell in behind the members with Radar bringing up the rear. Red seemed unaffected by the weight of his load and led the group at a brisk pace that kept me out of breath. As we approached the slide, there were other members emerging from the cave and they all lined up standing in the rocks above the opening in an eerie quiet procession of silence. There were some members that I hadn't seen before. I counted close to thirty members in all. Seeing them in the daylight revealed many different shapes and sizes, all of which made for a strong and healthy-looking tribe.

Elder stood by the entrance of the cave and waited for the members to come out. Grumpy was standing in the rocks looking proud and strong for her age, she was truly a force all her own. Elder stepped down into the slide area and Red took his position on the large flat rock. He brought his shouldered male down and cradled him in his arms like a child in front of his body. I stayed back out of the rocks and watched as the entire tribe looked at Red for some sign as to what to do next.

Scarface stood just above Red with Raspberry at his side looking bewildered and curious. With all eyes on Red, the large male stood tall and strong for a moment and looked sadly at the lifeless male in his arms. After a few seconds, Red tilted his head back and howled up at the sky with the most lonesome scream. The sound broke the silence with a resounding echo that lasted forever throughout the mountain range and sent shivers down my spine. It was loud and heart wrenching as it embodied the sorrow and mourning of one experiencing a great loss.

I couldn't help but get caught up in the emotion of the procession and my heart weighed heavy inside my own chest for the loss this tribe was enduring. The members all lined up throughout the slide and stood with respect as Red echoed one more scream. Tears trickled down the sides of his cheekbones past his square jaw and fell onto his broad chest. Looking out at the rest of his tribe, Red finished as he blew out his air and let out a final, sad groan from deep within his chest. I was mesmerized by the community grief and watched in awe at the way the entire tribe shared the pain. For a primitive group, their display of affection, grief and unity was unparalleled.

What happened next, revealed one of the greatest secrets and amazing customs showing the loyalty and cohesion within the tribe. One by one, the each began to pick up a stone from the slide and place it out on the grassy area. Everyone, no matter how big or small, young or old, continued to pick up a stone from the slide and carry it down the hill and stack it on the growing pile in the grass. They were all picking from the same area high up within the slide and the incredible excavation began. Red remained alone, standing on the flat rock near the entry point of the cave. He continued cradling the younger male in his arms looking tired and heartbroken, yet strong and astute. Not sure of my role, I stepped forward to help the rest and carry stones from the slide.

Scarface hissed at me and growled loudly, advancing aggressively towards me. I immediately stepped back from the slide and quickly retreated back into the grassy area which seemed to satisfy Scarface enough to resume his work on the slide.

After about an hour of work, there was an enormous cavity within the slide area that was easily twenty five or thirty-feet deep. With the continuous labor of thirty-some members, the amount of unified work accomplished compared to nothing I had ever seen. From my vantage point I could see the dirt on the bottom level, but as the stones were removed I started seeing bones and a skull from a past burial. Within minutes there were several skulls that were so close to human in appearance, except for the sheer size and a slightly longer forehead.

With many bones exposed on the ground, I noticed something that caught my eye. It was a pair of pants and what looked like a buckskin shirt with bones inside. The skull was still under some stones, but the boots were still intact. I could only guess that whoever had been involved with these creatures in the past had meant enough to the tribe to warrant being buried in the slide with the rest.

I watched in fascination the efficiency at which these primal members worked, realizing that we could learn from this tribe what it means to work together. All the members had lined up again along the inside edge of the opening that they had just created. Again, all eyes were on Red as he turned away from the opening to come down to the area where the others had gathered. He walked slowly by the entire tribe, and one by one they reached out to touch the face of the young deceased male as he was carried by. The amazing display of affection within the tribe made them look like a family.

Red had carried this young male from the time he took his last breath, either on his shoulders or in his arms for roughly four hours without ever letting him touch the ground. As he stepped beyond Scarface, who was the last in line, Red accepted his assistance as they gingerly placed the male among the other remains. With their backs to us they both rose, standing side by side they looked down at the male with a calm quietness in the air. Red reached out and touched the elbow of his companion, and they both turned and exited the open cavity.

Red resumed his position above the burial ground on his flat rock by the cave entrance, while the rest of the members again began to move all the stones back into the large void. Stone by stone, all were placed back on top of the tribe's deceased. Within an hour and a half, the area was completely filled back in without so much as one small stone remaining in the grass. With the last stone placed on the slide, Red turned and disappeared into the cave's entrance. All members, single file, headed back into the entrance of the cave leaving me staring at the rock slide that looked as it always had. Amazed and impressed with the entire funeral, I was again left alone in the open grassy area to do as I pleased. I could think of nothing I wanted more than to lie on my back in the small bed in the cabin and rest for the night.

The Pack

With the tribe preparing for the winter months and stocking up on game, I came to realize I needed to get some preparing done for myself. I started by picking out a couple of deer skins that looked intact and began the grueling process of scraping the flesh. This made them soft and pliable for brain tanning. Once the flesh and hair was removed from the hides, I soaked them in a brain and water solution for a day while I prepared a rack to stretch the skin over for the final drying scrape. My activities had me occupied and so busy that I was unaware of my audience, Radar, who was just beside himself with curiosity. He watched attentively through the entire process, as if trying to learn a new skill for his bag of tricks. With the two hides stretched out, I began to scrape both sides in an attempt to force out the moisture, which is a time consuming and exhausting activity.

Gingerly picking up one of my sharp-edged scraping stones, Radar tried to imitate my actions. I slowed down and started from the center, scraping from the center of the hide in an outward sweep and making a point to exaggerate the method. Radar followed suit but started from the edge working inward, which would have kept the moisture within the hide. I stopped and slowly put my stone on the hide he had chosen to work with. I placed my hand on his wrist to have him follow my movements. He tensed up and became very rigid at the contact on his wrist, but I patiently kept my hand soft and gentle, moving my hand from the center towards the outside. He seemed to grasp what I meant and withdrew his hand. He put the stone in his other hand, placing it in the center of the hide and swept in the outward motion, as if it was his own idea and intention. This was the first time I had actually reached out and touched one of the tribe members.

I stepped back and went back to work on my other hide. I watched out of the corner of my eye as Radar continued to mimic my movements, actually pushing the moisture to the outside of the skin. Switching back and forth from front to back, it took a couple of hours to complete the hide that I was working on, but the leather came through and the skin fluffed up into a nice smooth hide. I looked at the skin Radar was still laboring on and saw that it too was a smooth, fine piece of leather. I stepped back and set my stone down to inspect the skins one last time. I noticed several other tribe members were comfortably sitting by the brush watching Radar and I working together.

It was a class and instruction on tanning, and Radar was my star pupil. Untying the hides, I cut away some of the rough and hard edges that couldn't be reached in the final scraping process. I had in my hands two nicely done blankets for the winter months ahead. I put one over my shoulder, stepped forward and handed the second one to Radar who was surprised at the smoothness of the hide. He gently rubbed it on his face to feel its softness. He seemed very proud, and his eyes gave away his appreciation as he turned to the others to go back to his cave with his bounty thrown over his own shoulder. I watched as several members stood up, now that class was over, and was pleasantly surprised to see Scarface and Red stand up from their dark corner of the trees and head back towards the cave.

Radar, who was about twenty yards away suddenly stopped and blew out his breath loudly while staring downhill through the clearing below the slide area trees. His warning caught the undivided attention of the others as Red picked up his pace and came to Radar's side, also setting his gaze towards the other side of the clearing. Scarface came in quickly behind while I watched the others come out to where the three stood. All had their attention towards the other side of the clearing. A little movement caught my eye as two large, mangy wolves came into view which brought a low growl from deep within Red. The wolves were big with their low, head swinging movement that never seemed to still. As the two trotted closer with their nervous back and forth heads towards our position, several more wolves appeared in the clearing behind them. A few more fell in behind with their long, gangling gait. The two front runners stopped short, catching the attention of the rest of the pack. They brought their heads up high as they smelled and saw several tribe members in front of them.

With all the wolves in the clearing, sixteen in all, not one of them was smooth and attractive but instead rough, and scruffy. They were all light grey in color except a small, mangy, dark-haired wolf that looked almost black. Their eyes were beady and mean as bared their long pronounced canine teeth at the tribal members. Their big, cumbersome feet looked awkward as their long legged, bouncy gait made their fur move wildly in the wind.

Unaware of the situation at hand, Raspberry came around the bottom of the rock slide, heading up the trail towards our location with her little back towards the dangerous pack that stood attentively watching her. Scarface sprung into motion immediately as he and Red lunged towards her. With the wolves closer to her than Scarface and Red, one of the wolves rushed forward and embraced the opportunity before him. As if caught in the momentum of the rushing wolf, the others quickly followed, closing the gap on the still unaware Raspberry. Scarface bared his teeth and let out a snarl that stopped Raspberry in her tracks. Raspberry looked back and saw the dangerous pack closing in on her. With a scream, she started to run awkwardly towards the safety of Scarface and Red who were bearing down on her location. I watched in amazement as the two large males covered the distance with the speed of

Olympic runners. For the sheer size of Red and Scarface, they moved smoothly with tremendous power and grace as they closed the distance to Raspberry in seconds.

It was Scarface who reached Raspberry first. I watched as she leapt high in the air into his arms and circled up to the safety of his shoulders and back where she clung to his neck with both arms, wrapping her legs around his midsection. His hands free and Red at his side, they veered off towards the cave just a few feet ahead of the excited wolves. Lunging and snapping at the feet and calves of Red they pursued the runners as they deftly navigated the rocks towards the entrance. The rocks were a tough terrain for the wolves, so Scarface and Red were able to advance to the entrance well ahead of the pursuing pack. As they ducked inside, the wolves stopped short of the entrance, cautious of what might be waiting inside. They stood on the flat rock with their nervous side to side movements.

The few short seconds this took to play out was fascinating and had my adrenaline pumping. I looked around and found I was standing alone. Where all the tribe members had vanished to, I had no idea. Not wanting to be attacked by the wolves myself, I backed away from the cabin and headed for a large pine tree that went up about eighty or ninety feet. I figured from that height, there was no way the wolves could get to me. As I approached I saw three tribe members in the same tree. I was grateful when one of the male members came down to pull me up the first ten feet and put me above his position. Like a jungle tree full of chimps, we all got comfortable and waited within the safety of our tree. Holding our positions for an hour we waited for the pack to move on. Finally we watched them leave over the flat area above the cabin and past the glacier. Once again, the male assisted me by carefully bringing me back down the tree to the safe ground below. I felt like they were showing me courtesy and protecting me. I didn't know why, but I accepted and appreciated it.

Special Delivery

One early afternoon, there was a commotion that had the tribe scrambling and moving towards the cave and Red shuffled towards me with an expression that made me uneasy. As he came closer, he gave a bark, like that of a large dog, followed by a loud noisy blowing of his breath through his pursed lips. That caught the attention of Radar who was just coming back from the glacier. He changed his direction and headed straight towards me, almost at a run, which really got me nervous as the look on his face was that of sheer panic. Whatever those two communicated to each other was serious and had both members coming towards me in great haste. Red got to me first and I braced myself for the worst as he reached out and grabbed my elbow. To my surprise he was gentle while he tugged at me to follow him towards the cave. His face had an odd and nervous expression as if he had bad news for me.

There was no one in sight as we entered the cave, but the powerful stench of nasty hygiene was very much present. We passed through the cave, beyond the running water, and out into the final opening. Several members were crowded around one female member who was lying prone on the floor, moving about in pain. I immediately saw she was pregnant and was clearly having some serious difficulties birthing her baby. I knew nothing of childbirth or what to do in the situation, and I was puzzled as to why I was brought to witness this particular event. I had no desire to be in this rancid smelling cave with these hygiene deficient giants and witness the birth of a little baby Bigfoot.

I took a half step backwards only to bump into Radar who was making certain that I did not go anywhere. Confused, I looked towards Radar for some kind of indication when suddenly the young female on the floor noticed me in the room and began to hiss loudly. She screamed towards me, "John Stone! John Stone!" Now this had my undivided attention, and chills ran up and down my spine like never before in my life. Did I hear that right? My question was answered in an instant with another "John Stone!" All the other members seemed to be looking in my direction, putting me on the spot and making me more uncomfortable. I was amazed by the clear words coming from the mouth of this female member. I had no idea what to do or say, but understood this female had plenty of practice with these words. She was also truly in some serious trouble lying on the dirt floor trying to give birth to this baby. I didn't know what I was doing, but I stepped towards her and knelt down close on the hard ground.

She immediately reached out and grabbed my hand, pulling me close so she could get a close look at my face. She was definitely different from the rest. From the size of her body, shape of her face and overall appearance of her skin, she certainly had a completely different look. Just gazing at her face with her long eyelashes, square jaw line, high cheekbones and virtually no hair on her face, she was what I would call attractive, almost pretty. She had much less hair on her body, and she had curvier, womanly features through her arms and legs. She didn't look like she was any more than six feet tall.

Hey, wait a minute, did I just think to myself that she was 'almost pretty?' I haven't been up here long enough for that kind of delusion, but she was indeed an attractive female member. She had more features of a human female than any other member of the tribe that I had seen, not to mention the fact she had just spoken the words, "John Stone," in a very human tone. My head was spinning as I tried to take it all in and determine whether this was some kind of messed up dream playing itself out in my sleep.

I looked around and saw Grumpy kneeling down with the female and positioned by her knees so she could assist in the birth of the newborn. Her personality had not improved since our first meeting, and she glared at me with absolute disgust and disapproval. The others were all standing around with mild curiosity and more focused on my presence than the female in pain. It occurred to me this female was young, like that of a college age girl by comparison to the older female at her side. Although she appeared different than the rest, it looked as if no one in the tribe made the comparison or looked at her any differently than any other member.

Her breathing quickened and her grip on my hand intensified as she began to push and arch her back in discomfort. Grumpy leaned in and reach for the grand entrance of the new tribe member as the breach began. As much as I didn't want to be there, I couldn't help but watch in amazement as I witnessed my first childbirth of what appeared to be a hairless human looking baby boy. The other members seemed to be curious by the pink, hairless newborn baby and crept in for a closer look. Grumpy hissed a little louder and barked out a few sounds that emptied the room in an instant. She didn't seem to notice that the newborn was different and held it close as it wailed against her chest. She gently lifted the newborn boy and looked at it with soft eyes filled with kindness. She put the baby's soft bald head to her cheek and lips with affection.

The female holding my hand released her grip and reached out to the older woman, wanting to touch her new prize. I couldn't take my eyes off the baby and watched in amazement as the new mother held her son close to her face with soft gentle whispers of "John Stone." The older female stroked the head of the younger female and gently touched the face of the new baby. For an instant, they both looked happy and there appeared to be almost a smile on Grumpy's face. Then she looked up at me with her sizzling expression, which was my cue to leave. As I stood up to make my exit, the new mother reached back to my arm and pulled me down to the ground again. With gentle hands, she held onto my hand for support and what seemed to be validation. I got comfortable and leaned against her arm and shoulder, which seemed to give her comfort for some reason. Grumpy watched our movements closely and relaxed enough to show her allowance of my presence, for now.

I was wearing an over shirt that I had found in the cabin, so I removed it and placed it on top of the baby and partially on his mother. She released her hold on my arm and took an interest in the shirt. Feeling like I was off the hook for now, I stood slowly and exited the large room, past the water and out the front entrance to the pure wonderful fresh air and brilliant sunlight. I felt honored to have witnessed the birth of a new tribe member and was still spinning from the clarity of the words spoken in the cave.

It was becoming more difficult to look at these members without seeing their personalities and finding a more human side to them every day.

Stealth and Grace

I left the cabin intending to head to the glacier and do a little washing of my face as well as a few clothes that had somehow gotten dirty and smelled of sweat and filth. When I came out into the open, I saw Raspberry in the brush crawling like a cat ready to pounce on its prey with expert skill. This had me curious to see what she was up to. I set down my belongings at the door, stepped back into the cabin, and leaned my back against its stout walls and watched the game of cat and mouse play itself out in front of me.

Her curious eyes were fixed on something in the ground in front of her. Not more than ten feet away, she was down on all fours with her feet dug in so she could lunge ahead towards whatever it was that had her attention. Looking into the dirt I could see a small hole in the dusty earth that maybe a small rodent occupied as its safe haven from the predators flying the skies above. Having no idea of the imminent danger that lurked outside waiting to pounce at the very sight of its fur, a small field mouse emerged from its protective hole and looked towards my direction in full view.

Looking beyond him, I saw Raspberry rock her hip to the side in preparation for what I'm sure was going to be a ferocious, breathtaking attack. She tensed up like a spring and sprung forward, surprisingly without a sound, high into the air. With her hands outstretched and teeth bared she displayed furrowed brows and mean, focused eyes. In the air she looked vicious and ready for the battle of taking down her prey at any cost. Her knobby knees were slightly bent and the hair on her back rose in true warrior form.

The idea was well thought out. The determination was there to prepare, plan and execute this dangerous hunt. Half way through the gravity-defying leap, though, she realized that ten feet was too much distance to travel in her limited power. She came crashing down hard, missing her target by a mere three feet which gave the formable adversary adequate time and distance to retreat back into the sanctuary of its home. Without missing a beat, Raspberry was leaping for the hole and pushed her skinny fingers inside; hoping to redeem what was left of her failed attempt. Pulling the loose dirt to the side, she burrowed deeper with her face in the now dusty remains of a hole to sniff out the culprit that had somehow escaped her well executed attack. Not giving up so easily she dug the dirt away and burrowed her face in even deeper into the fresh dirt for even a remnant of flavor from the elusive and speedy escapee.

I must have inhaled too loudly from my suppressed laughter because I startled the sleek brave hunter. Quickly she spun her head around in a puff of dust, contrasting her dark face with the light powdered dust that adorned her wet nose and eyes. She was squinting and blinking her eyes trying to remove the irritating bits of dirt and debris. As she tried focusing on me she spit out her tongue to make her trademark raspberry sound, but the dirt in her mouth made the sound more of a hiss. Laughing out loud now, I took in the pitiful sight of the dusty tongued, raccoon faced, knobby kneed, eye blinking hunter as she tried bravely to regain her dignity. Frustrated and defeated by the elusive field mouse, she defiantly shuffled out of the dirt towards the sanctuary of her own rock-slide fortress.

Poking its head out of the small hole, the field mouse watched her exit the area and with a fierce battle cry squeak, turned and dove back into its safe haven.

Clues on the Summit

Jeff and Vic spent the morning on the main trail, and as the sounds of rushing water faded, they began the steep climb into the afternoon getting over the summit where the last known campsite was for Turley. When they approached the small rock slide, their pace slowed as they looked for leftover signs that hadn't been erased by the initial law enforcement that had been called to the scene. Knowing the tree was the central point, they understood that this would be the most trampled up space. Even so, Jeff knelt down to where the blood was and started inspecting the area closely. "Hmm, well that doesn't surprise me."

"What have you got there, Jeff?" Vic asked.

"Not too sure yet, but it might give us some idea," Jeff replied. "It looks like we have two kinds of blood here."

"Oh really?" Vic questioned. "Let me see what you have."

"If you look at the blood that is deep in the soil, you have almost a burgundy color as it dried up. Now right here there is a smaller pool of blood where the color is almost black. No matter how deep the wound, the color would maintain the same once it dried up." Jeff continued, "This is a much different color, and I'm finding it impossible to think that they came from the same source. It looks like your boy might have put up a bit of a fight before it was all finished. The question is, which pool of blood belongs to him?"

"I would like to think that it is the smaller of the two," Vic grinned grimly at his buddy. "From the photos, the shell casing was right here by the second source of blood that you found. My only guess is that the shot was at close range and the casing was unable to go very far."

"Did your Sheriff buddy mention that there might have been two sources of blood?" Jeff asked.

"No, I think they might have missed that one," Vic responded with a sarcastic tone.

"You said there were four of them and that they spent a whole day up here and they found nothing at all?" Jeff asked with equal sarcasm.

"Clean shirt, city folks!" Vic said wryly.

Jeff continued to circle the camp in clean methodical patterns, periodically lying on his chest inspecting something in the dirt or a pattern left in the pine needles of something that passed but seemed to have left no obvious tracks.

Vic did his own searching below the camp and even further down past the cliffs for any signs of evidence that might give them a clue of what took place on the mountain. Suddenly, Jeff let out a quick whistle that got Vic's attention and brought him back up above the rock slide where Jeff was lying on his chest again.

"If you're not too tired old man, why don't you come down here with me and get some perspective on what happened," Jeff invited with a curious grin.

"Oh my, I'm afraid that in my condition, I may not be able to get back up from that position without the help of a come-along," Vic poked back. "Tell me what we're looking at."

As Vic dropped to the ground, he placed the side of his face on the cool ground and looked over the vast area of pine needles from a level playing field. He could see a set of long, broad, indentation tracks that came to the edge of the upper rock slide, and a second set of the same long broad tracks moving away within a few feet of the first set. They were single placement footprints, like those of a man walking across the open area except they were a long stride that would be almost impossible for a man to follow. The tracks were a wide and indistinct pattern showing no edges, hooves or even claw marks to give it more than a large scale smudge. Seeing the look on Vic's face, Jeff let out a chuckle, "Got you a little confused, don't it?"

"Any chance of a pro basketball player out here with oversized shoes on, traipsing around these parts?" Vic quizzed.

"Not too likely Vic. My opinion is not going to hold water with you because what I'm thinking is something I know you'll scoff at," Jeff replied.

"What on earth do you mean by that, buddy? This could be the lead that we're looking for to find my son. I'm ready to hear whatever you've got," Vic replied.

"Vic, I have only seen this kind of track two times in my whole life and both times has led to more questions than answers." Jeff continued, "Once was higher up Kootenai Mountain about two miles from here in the 90's late in the fall. The tracks I found were just like this with no patterns or hard details, yet they were heavy from some serious weight pressing down. Come here and look at how this print is a bit deeper on this end where it has the deepest pressure. Now if you look at your own footprint, the front of the print is deeper as you roll onto your toes and push off when you step forward. These tracks are the same as ours and the forward part is the deepest where it will roll forward and push off with its toes. Even the single print stride and gait is exactly like ours. The part that you don't want to hear is that I have never seen what or who makes these tracks. There are some campfire stories that lean toward an explanation of what it is. Now I'm the kind of guy that has to see it and feel it for myself to believe it, but in this case, until I am shown otherwise, I still hold the opinion that it could be real."

"For Pete's sake, Jeff, you're talking in circles and are getting more confusing with time. Just give me the straight like you always have," Vic interrupted impatiently.

"I think that a Sasquatch or Bigfoot made these tracks Vic," Jeff said solemnly. "I know you have always dismissed the whole idea and scoffed at all the wild stories, but unless you have a better idea than a pro basketball player with oversized feet, we will have to run with my theory for the time being," Jeff blurted out.

After a short pause, Vic pulled off his hat and wiped off his forehead. "In all serious-ness Jeff, I have known you for most of your life. I have always trusted you through the best and the worst of it. I will give you this one for now until we have more tangible evidence to work with, but so help me Jeff, if you go running into town telling folks that I am looking for a Bigfoot that abducted my boy, you will make me the laughing stock of the entire county. This crazy Bigfoot theory stays between us and us alone; no wife, no friends, no sheriff and I mean nobody, OK?" Vic asked.

"You're my best friend Vic. I would only make myself look crazier than you due to the fact that I'm the one helping you look for your Bigfoot-abducted boy, and yes, of course you have my word," Jeff replied seriously.

They both rose up from the ground and began following the difficult trail. It appeared that whatever it was that they were following seemed to seek out the rocks and avoid traveling upon the soft earth.

Lost in the Water

Jeff led the way through the dense trees and thick undergrowth until he stopped abruptly beside a flat-leafed bush and turned back with a huge grin on his face.

"Check this out Vic, I knew they were traveling together but just couldn't put my finger on it," Jeff announced.

"You see how there is blood on this top leaf? Well look at this lower leaf, it has a drip and a smudge on it. Now," Jeff said plucking the upper leaf, "look at the two side by side."

As Vic inspected the two blood samples together, it was obvious they were very different in color and from two different sources.

"Jeff, we're following only one set of tracks with two entirely different blood types, how do suppose both types got here in the same spot unless one is being carried?" Vic asked

"That's the only way it could be Vic. You see these tracks are much heavier on the left side to indicate that it is limping or carrying, or even both," Jeff responded. "Obviously the one being carried is your son, and without proof of what is carrying him I have to believe that it is something on two feet. It's got to be something big and definitely strong enough to climb these inclines without breaking a stride. These tracks are easily eighteen to twenty inches long, and a good eight to ten inches wide by the center of the indents. It looks like there is something wider and longer on the print to make it impossible to get an exact size, maybe some kind of shoe or covering."

"As long as we have a trail and enough track to identify direction let's keep following. I'm going to guess that we've come at least five or six miles, through some rough country." Vic continued, "I've not seen any indication of the tracks stopping, resting or even slowing down. Heck, we're almost all the way up to the lower side of the lake."

As the two continued on they came to a wide crossing in the creek. They were about a mile from South Kootenai Lake where the tracks went into the water but did not come out the other side. The tracks that led up to it were not directed uphill or downhill. It seemed as if they hit the water and disappeared. "Oh that's just plain rotten. Vic, you see these tracks could go either direction. I think this thing used the water to make a conscious choice to cover its trail. We could go up or down, it's your choice buddy and we'll each take a side and comb the bank for tracks," Jeff explained.

"Well, let's go down a short distance and unless we find anything in the next hour, I think we should break for the night. I'm thinking fresh trout would be an appropriate dinner after our first big day out," Vic said with a sigh.

After an hour of detailed search the two looked at each other across the water and with a nod, took off their packs on a small little patch of flat ground for the night. Vic pulled in two fairly large trout and one medium 'pan size' that made for two full bellies for the tired trackers that night.

"Jeff, you mentioned you saw these kinds of tracks twice. What about the second time, what did you find?" Vic asked.

"I was on a late elk hunt in the Clearwater area about eight or nine years ago and kept getting that feeling that I was being watched," Jeff began, "you know that feeling?"

"Yes I do, it's not a good thing," Vic answered.

"Well something had spooked the elk, and they were scattering out of an upper basin like cockroaches in the light when I spotted a five point bull coming my way. I settled in for my shot when the air filled with this stench that would make a gut pile seem like perfume. I squeezed off a shot that dumped the elk in the brush not more than a hundred yards away, a good clean shot. The kind of shot you have confidence in," Jeff continued.

"I had to drop down into a small draw and come up to where the elk dropped, but when I got there the elk had disappeared. Something had dragged the bull about fifty feet. Now we're talking within ten minutes of my shot. There were tons of prints like we have right here. Then the drag marks just vanished as if it was picked up and carried out."

"Carried the entire elk? Now how is that possible?" Vic wondered in amazement.

"I saw where it went down. I even saw where it bled out for a bit before it was drug away. There must have been eight or ten sets of these tracks in that area that came in from the north and left the same way loaded down with something really heavy. Vic, those tracks were just like these right here that we have been following. They vanished into a creek just like this one did. I was never able to pick up on the trail after that. Have to tell you though; I have never smelled anything like that before in my life. It was the first time in my life I was glad to leave the woods and drive away in my truck. That was the first time I ever questioned the existence of Bigfoot or whatever it is that they call it."

Needing rest for the continued search the next day, the two friends turned in for the night, with no more talk of the legendary Bigfoot.

The Grudge

There was light snow on the ground, it was late September by now and the clouds were becoming more frequent. The high country was going to get its first heavy snow cover soon. With all the supplies being gathered and meat being brought in, I got the idea that it would soon be hibernation time and the tribe would settle for several months within the protection of the cave.

Scarface and Radar approached the cabin with a nice bold stride that appeared to be almost cheerful and carefree. While Scarface stood outside, the young fearless male came in and literally plopped down on the bed with that anxious appearance of 'let's go play' look on his face. I stood up, and grabbed an over shirt as Radar stepped past me and exited the cabin looking for me to come with him.

This time we didn't head for the cave but started uphill to the glacier and beyond it. We had never gone this way before. The direction was new to me as we made our way across the creek, around the glacier and out past the distant ridge line. Once we dropped down past the ridge, we traveled about a mile to find Red standing there looking out over the range with a distant look in his eyes, not moving, just smelling the air.

As we approached, Red blew out a loud sound that was serious enough to stop Scarface in his tracks. Radar did the same. I watched as all three smelled the air paying close attention to the appearance of Red and the dark red color on his head, neck and back. He looked like a dog with its hair raised just before it would growl and warn of a possible attack. Scarface stepped in closer to Red and stood beside him with the same statuesque posture. Both sensed some kind of danger and were on high alert.

Seeing the two standing there reminded me of two best friends who had been through every adventure together, with plenty more on the horizon. The hair on Scarface's back rose and Radar became anxiously restless and headed back towards the glacier again. Radar clearly wanted nothing to do with whatever it was that these two had wind of and chose the right idea to leave the area. Glad to follow, I stepped in behind him to make our way back to familiar ground when Scarface sounded a command and stopped Radar short.

Red growled low and heavy with long sustained tones that seemed to last forever with each breath. His tones were not directed at us but towards the tree line just above us to our left. Scarface too stared at the tree line with intensity. Red started moving to the left and upwards towards the spot that had caught his eye, when I heard something in the trees blow loudly followed by the sound of something hitting the base of a tree several times. It wasn't the sound of an antler, but the sound of hands or feet of soft flesh striking the hard surface of the tree. The loud blowing sound was the same sound that came from Red and Scarface in the past when they were on high alert status. Radar's eyes were wide with fear and dread.

Taking it all in, I knew that something bad was in the making and with Red and Scarface's reaction I had the feeling that I was in a bad spot. Radar moved in behind Scarface and I followed closely, not wanting to get separated from my mountain guides. As we came in behind Red, I noticed some movement in the trees above. I couldn't tell exactly what it was because it looked dark in the shadows. The ground was fairly level where we were, and the trees were getting thinner along with the brush and undergrowth. Straining my eyes to see what it was, I wondered if we had come upon a Grizzly or some kind of mountain lion as I couldn't think of anything else that would put these creatures on edge like this. Suddenly I saw movement to our left, but Red was fixed on something just to the right of it, maybe a sow with cubs, which could be a recipe for disaster for sure. Still unsure of what was ahead, Radar and I both kept back about ten feet from Scarface and Red. Red's growling was getting louder and more intense as we came into a clear area about half the size of a football field. Roughly fifteen feet into the clearing Red stopped short and Scarface came up to stand beside him, both with hair on their necks and back standing on end.

Red was blowing loudly and showing more signs of irritation, and his movements were becoming aggressive. He then stepped forward and took his open right hand and hit his own chest, as his left hand hit his left thigh with a resounding crack that echoed through the valley. The scene before me looked more primal and apelike in behavior than I had seen yet from these creatures. Again he growled low and slapped his chest and thigh with an echoing crack as the two stood poised as if ready for battle.

Radar stepped closer to me with his shoulder and elbow touching me, as if the feeling of me near gave him comfort. There was another loud blow from just out of sight, followed by a low deep growl that ended with a sharp snarl and the sounds of teeth snapping open and shut. This only seemed to infuriate Red even more as his own growl became louder and the slapping started to come at a faster pace. The rhythmic echoes closed in on one another. Standing out in the open, I was amazed at how calm and quiet Scarface stood through all of this open display of rage. His only response was his raised hair throughout his back making him look as large and solid as a rock monument. Everything suddenly stopped, and there was an eerie heaviness in the air as the echoes lingered and faded away leaving behind a heavy silence. Even the breeze that was once in the air waited to see what was going to happen next, as if nature was on hold for this battle to play itself out.

Like three shadowy ghosts coming out from under the shade of the trees, there appeared three beasts walking single file from the other side of the clearing. These three were not familiar to me and had not been part of the tribe where I had been staying these past weeks. The one in the lead was pure black and obviously the Alpha male of the three given his size and presentation. He was easily the same size as Scarface, maybe even a little bit larger and was an impressive beast.

His hair was shiny, and from his back to the top of his head he had a strip of hair that was a couple of inches longer than the rest. It had the look of a Mohawk and gave him an intimidating appearance. His eyes were not small and evil, but rather big and alert with a solid pronounced brow line that offered good protection. With a flat, broken nose of a boxer and the jaw line made of tempered steel, this male was clearly the best in show from his tribe. He was thick throughout the chest and had well developed arms that showed off strong veins throughout his hairy body. As if chiseled from black granite, he walked proud and tall with defiance and stared with hatred at Red.

Silently, they moved closer and not once did the large lead male take his fixed stare off of Red. As the Alpha male stopped ten feet away from Red, the other two stepped in beside him in a wall of massive flesh and power. The standoff was exciting as well as frightening with the monstrous large male squaring off with Red in an intense, iron-grip gaze. The other two males looked equally ferocious never taking their eyes off of me, which made me feel uneasy and awkward. One of the males staring at me started to move in my direction with intent in his eyes that didn't look friendly.

As he neared, Scarface lunged to the side and placed his massive body between us and slapped his own chest and thigh, with a deep, throaty growl dropping his giant wide open hands to his sides and flexing his knees to embrace his opponent's possible attack.

Seeing it wouldn't be so easy to deal with me alone, the male hesitated, and the large black Alpha barked out a quick sound that had the confrontational male scrambling back to his position beside the other male. As Scarface straightened up, he stiffly walked back over to stand beside Red who had not moved an inch.

With another blow and bark from Alpha, the two male members both obediently stepped back about four steps. Scarface also followed suit and stepped back and positioned himself between Red and where Radar and I were standing. This left Alpha and Red standing to face each other with the rest of us out of the way. It looked as if there was some bad history between Alpha and Red and it was up to them alone to sort it out. The respect for the two enemies was abided by all parties involved. Watching Scarface and the two large males stepping back was fascinating. It appeared as if they followed a code within their species that was understood and not questioned.

Red wasted no time as he leapt forward with a fierce growl and ran his shoulder into the chest and chin of his nemesis, sprawling him onto the flat ground. The sound of the impact was loud and I could actually feel the ground vibrate from the large Alpha hitting the earth just a few feet away. As the male hit the ground on his back, Red followed him down and wrapped his giant hands around the thick neck of his opponent landing on Alpha's chest with his weight. The black male turned his head to the left with his bright white teeth bared and snapped at Red's wrist. Red let go and jerked back just in time to miss the snapping jaws. This offered an opportunity for Alpha to continue his turn and roll himself onto his knees and spring to his feet with his back still to Red.

Straightening up and off balance, Alpha had not turned all the way around before Red charged into the waist of the male, wrapping his huge arms around the larger black male. Picking Alpha high off the ground to his shoulders, Red turned and thrust him back down to the ground hard onto his head and shoulders, then pounced on the Alpha. Seeing that fighting move reminded me of something I had experienced for myself and I winced remembering that it was a very unpleasant way to meet the earth.

This time Alpha was stunned but still ready for Red's attack, and he circled his hands around Red's neck and shoulder drawing him in close. Red pulled away quickly but not before Alpha had locked his teeth into the left side of Red's neck and shoulder, deep into the flesh below. Unable to break free from the locked jaws, Red was caught in the grip of his opponent.

Red's blood began oozing from his neck and around the mouth of Alpha making the violent scene before me one of the fiercest fights I had ever encountered. Using his only option, Red grabbed Alpha's right arm with both hands and yanked it down towards the ground. He pulled his knee up against the side of the elbow and concentrated all his force on the joint. With Alpha's teeth deep in the side of his thick neck, Red strained against the thick, dense elbow joint and felt it start to give way under the intense pressure. Realizing his elbow was going to be compromised, Alpha released his teeth from Red's neck and let go with his good arm to grab at his hand and support the elbow.

The attempt to save his elbow was a little too late in coming and a loud pop came from underneath the skin as the joint became displaced and shifted out of its socket. Alpha let out a hoarse scream of agony that drew no attention or reaction from the others.

As I glanced up from the primitive fight before me I saw no emotion, tension or interest from the other members, only unattached waiting for the completion of the event. Radar was the only face that showed anything. He was consumed by the conflict and appeared more frightened than anything else. Scarface looked back and forth between the activity on the ground and the two males who stood by watching emotionless as the fight continued.

With blood pushing from the open wound on Red's neck, Alpha again sank his teeth into Red's right shoulder and tore back the flesh with a violent shake of his head. His teeth gleaming with fresh blood, he drove his head once again towards Red's throat only to be met by the elbow of Red, knocking Alpha's head back and forcing him to the ground. Red again jumped on his opponent with fury and speed as he drove his knees into Alpha's neck. Red quickly grabbed the dislocated elbow and twisted it violently, tearing the tendons inside. The agonizing pain made Alpha turn away from Red, putting his chest into the dirt trying to escape the pain radiating from his elbow.

Red threw his leg over Alpha and climbed onto his back and locked both arms around the neck of the large male. This choke put Alpha into a twisting and turning motion to escape from the steel grip of the bleeding male on his back. As both rolled together on the ground, Alpha's eyes turned red and bloodshot from the sheer pressure Red was putting on his throat. Red drove his face into the side of the neck of the large black male, burying his teeth deep into the soft exposed flesh, pulling away the skin and opening up the blood flow. Alpha's mouth was open for a breath but no air was able to go in or out with Red's pressure on the closed wind pipe.

Red's hands were tight and white around the knuckles from the grip and energy he put into the chokehold. In a final panic, Alpha reached upwards and grabbed one of Red's hands and began to pry it away with all his strength. With his grip slipping, Red was unwilling to give up such a position without making Alpha pay. Red shifted his grip so he could bring his knee up into the ribs of the male and delivered two rib shattering blows before his grip gave way. As Alpha arched his back to strain against Red's grip, he was able to catch some breath and fight with a renewed energy. Managing to break free and roll to his knees, Alpha jumped up and turned to face his attacker.

Red was losing a lot of blood from his neck and shoulder and was showing signs of weakness. His red hide was becoming covered in his own blood. The wound from his shoulder was deep and I could see the muscles move beneath as he moved to face his adversary. Red rushed forward with his thick head low and drove it into the face of Alpha. Red's forehead collided with Alpha's teeth splitting his head wide open above his brow. The impact threw Alpha's head backwards and he began to fall as several teeth that were knocked loose fell from his upper jaw into the dirt. The momentum was too much for him as he tried to regain his footing. He ended up on his back in the dirt. Red met him on the ground, with both knees on top of the already shattered ribs and again grabbed at the broken elbow to twist his opponent onto his stomach. Red reached under his broken arm and around the back of his neck. Taking advantage of his new position and reaching with both arms, Red began to bear down with tremendous force on the back of Alpha's head.

The large alpha male had no retreat or position to escape as Red increased the pressure on the neck. I watched as blood pulsed from the side of Alpha's neck and his chin forced against his chest and off to the side. I could tell his neck was weakening under Red's tremendous power. With Red and the trapped male lying on their sides in the dirt, Red wrapped his legs around the male and applied every bit of strength into the grip on the neck of the larger beast. I watched as Red's back muscles began to knot up and his arms flexed with renewed power and determination of finishing this battle once and for all. With blood running down his face Red began to shake as the sheer force of his pressure required more strength. Alpha had been deprived of enough air and blood that he was unable to fight back any longer.

The sound that came next was like that of a small gunshot from beneath the surface of Alpha's shoulders as the neck finally surrendered to the relentless force. The large male was still and lifeless in the hands of an exhausted and bleeding Red. Everything was quiet, except for the heavy sounds of Red's breathing, as he removed his arm from beneath the fallen Alpha. Slowly Red rolled onto one knee, and Scarface stepped forward to pull him to his feet by his elbow. Scarface and the battle-scarred Red both stepped back and moved slowly out of the way from the fallen Alpha male.

Emotionless, the two males stepped forward with uncertainty. Not looking up at the four of us, one of the males reached down and hoisted Alpha up and positioned him on his broad shoulders. They both stood there for a second then turned to look back at us with cold, black beady eyes. With no change in their expressions they turned away and headed up the hill with their fallen member and continued out of sight.

Red was bleeding from his head, neck and chest and looked terrifying as he stared towards me with a hard, steely gaze. Unable to look away, I stared back in awe as he wiped away the fresh blood still escaping into his eyes and down his face. Even though exhausted and weak, he hadn't lost any of his fierce presence and sheer meanness as his eyes bored holes right through me.

I couldn't understand why he had so much animosity towards me, and I certainly hoped to never get him angry enough with me to put those giant crushing hands around my neck. With all the adrenaline that was still pulsing through his body, I hoped that wasn't what he was thinking right now as he continued to stare. It was Scarface who stepped forward and with his back to me walked between us and moved up the trail to head back towards our rock slide. Red turned and stepped in behind him. I followed with Radar right behind me.

Hatchet Man

Red was in bad shape for a while, and spent a fair amount of time either lying in the sunlight or trying to wash away the pain in the cool water from the stream. There was a look of content to his behavior, and he didn't seem to pay much attention to me, but when he did look in my direction I could tell that he still had issues with me being around.

Radar was around with Raspberry always under his feet. Their interaction was that of a brother and sister who continually antagonize one another. I wanted to work on some more of the animal skins and tan them for blanket materials for the cold months ahead. I picked out two more hides that were fairly fresh and started the process of scraping the flesh and hair off one of the hides.

Seeing that I was doing something familiar, Radar came over and began to imitate my actions by scraping the second hide I had picked out. With Radar close, Raspberry felt safe enough to come and curiously watch the entire process. I must give Radar credit for the detailed and thorough attention he gave to his work as he checked over his finished hide that was finally free of hair and excess flesh. The brain and water mix seemed to interest Raspberry the most while we mixed our tanning solution and placed the two freshly cleaned skins inside the old bucket of mix. The next morning, Radar was anxious to get started on the hanging and final stages of scraping the moisture from the hides and making the soft leather material. Again, the process took a couple of hours and the finish product was even better than the first two. I think Radar was getting the hang of the process and felt his own sense of accomplishment from the final product.

Without offering the second hide to Radar, he just picked it up and placed it over the shoulder of Raspberry and looked at me with that proud "look what I have done" gleam in his eye. Raspberry immediately grabbed it and started petting the soft material and put its softness to the side of her face. Excited and very proud of her new blanket, she turned and briskly headed for the cave's entrance to show it off. After the work invested in the hide, I was impressed at the unrestrained generosity Radar showed to Raspberry. This made me smile and gave me even more reason to believe that the two were closely related.

The very next day I came out of the cabin to find Radar waiting patiently outside with two more fresh hides, one elk hide and one deer hide with my bucket holding fresh brain materials needed for the job. Well, that decided it. *I guess I know what I'm doing today with my free time!*

I settled in for the task at hand when Scarface and a sore, still healing Red came up the hill with the telltale antler pieces in their hands. Radar understood this in an instant and laid the hides over top of the bucket and scurried away for his own antler. Scarface stopped him short communicated to him that he was not going this time.

The disappointment showed heavily on Radar's face as his shoulders slumped down in a pitiful fashion in a great display of pouting. To the two adult males it was a brilliant, but wasted, effort and not even noticed.

Scarface gave me a look that said nothing less than "let's get going slowpoke," which put me into motion. I pulled my shirt from off the top of a stump and stepped in behind Scarface. Red came in close behind us, and we headed back around the glacier where the confrontation between Red and Alpha had taken place. The memories of the area brought me no comfort as we passed over the side of the hill and directly through the clearing where the vicious fight happened. Scarface did not even acknowledge the area or hesitate as we stepped on the exact spot where Alpha had taken his last breath. It seemed that for them, the memory washed away as soon as we turned our backs and left. We journeyed out beyond the clearing, through an area of dense trees towards a distant rocky cliff that loomed in the distance. We moved in the same direction for the entire day and into the dark. My eyes couldn't adjust to the dark quick enough and I kept getting caught up in brush and branches that threatened to trip me. Red, noticing that I was stumbling in the dark, barked to Scarface from behind me causing Scarface to stop on the trail.

In the darkness I was unaware Scarface had actually stopped cold, until my chest and face planted into his back, which I don't think he was at all amused by. With darkness slowing me down, I was relieved when we made our way off the trail about a hundred feet and circled around a large pine to rest for the night. I am convinced that resting was for my benefit because I knew these creatures moved freely in the darkness. I hardly doubted that they were tired. I burrowed my way into a nice little dip in the root system that offered the cushion of needles and lower hanging pine boughs from the smaller trees nearby. As I settled in for a restless night's sleep, I could see the silhouette of the two adult male's simply leaning against the trees with their knees to their chest, resting their heads in their folded arms.

When I awoke, I could smell smoke from a fire in the distance and saw Red and Scarface still in their perspective spots, wide awake looking out towards our trail. Straightening my stiff legs before I got up, I caught the attention of the others and they rose to their feet almost immediately, ready to move on. Nature called and I turned my back on them to empty my bladder.

When I turned around, there was a look of disgust on Red's face as he turned towards the trail and stepped backwards waiting for me to step in behind the already moving Scarface. We followed the trail for about another mile, and I could see in the distance that there was a small amount of smoke rising indicating a human camp. Our approach was a wide half circle to the other side of the smoky area. It seemed as if we were walking straight towards the camp.

I had no idea why we were getting so close to a camp that was occupied by people, but I assumed the two giant males had a reason or a plan. As I stepped into a clear area, I was shocked to see that we had stepped out onto a gravel road. What road, I had no idea, but it was a well traveled, maintained forest service road with plenty of fresh tire tracks going in and out. Once we crossed the road I could see we were at a trailhead where the end of the gravel stopped and the beginning of a trail started. There was one single pickup truck in the distance with small puffs of smoke rising from a camp fire on the other side of it. Staying close to the trees, I watched as Scarface and Red crept closer to the camp making certain they made no sounds. The sign at the trailhead was faded and a little too far away to read its lettering to know where I was, but the shape of the sign was definitely an Idaho outline.

There were two sleeping bags on the ground close to a smoldering fire from the night before. There was trash from food, bottles, and empty cans of beer strewn all about the site. It sure gave an awful impression of campers in the west. I was, however, relieved to see that the plates on the truck were from another state, far away.

The sounds of snoring came loudly from both bags as the two were obviously sleeping off the previous nights festivities. Red boldly walked up to the truck, keeping the sleeping campers on the opposite side. Reaching in, he pulled two wool blankets from the open bed of the pickup. As he turned to walk away he stopped, turned back and reached in again and produced a small hatchet.

With two blankets and a hatchet in his hands, he backed away to our location, and the three of us moved towards the trail again. To my dismay we were on the wrong side of the trailhead sign for me to read the information. A half mile up the trail Scarface stopped and we all looked back over the trailhead at the messy camp. I had a hard time excusing the behavior of the out of state visitors. Even though they had been in party mode, I was embarrassed for how disrespectful of the wilderness they had been. Red, still holding the blankets, handed me the hatchet. It had looked tiny in his hands, yet it turned out to be fairly large and heavy, a good quality tool. It seemed that this was what we had come for and our mission was done. It seemed as if we were headed back for the base camp.

I wondered if this was something they did from time to time. Maybe they cased an area for whatever they could pick up or it could be that they had been here earlier and targeted these two partiers. In any case, I was happy to have the hatchet as it was a tool that I was familiar with. I wondered, why the blankets in particular? It was if he knew they were there.

Stone Wall

With Scarface leading, then me following and Red bringing up the rear, the pace back was fast and kept me almost at a half trot. I still could not get my bearings as to where I was except for the fact that we were somewhere in the Montana-Idaho territory. We were possibly floating back and forth over the state lines, not knowing whether it was the Nez Pierce or Clearwater National Forest.

I noticed Red's forehead was healing nicely, but the open tear on his shoulder was giving him pain and would periodically reopen and ooze blood which would then dry on the hair around the opening. His forearm still bled from two deep holes from the front teeth of Alpha. Red showed signs of pain, but not weakness, lack of power or energy. If it were me, I would need a month of lying on my back before I would even consider leaving the house. As human as his movements and appearance seemed to be, I was impressed at his ability to drive on in silence, despite his injuries.

Glancing back, it was an odd sight to see a beast like him carrying a couple of blankets under one arm and a huge piece of antler in the other hand. Red looked almost like he was heading out to his buddy's house for a sleep over with his blankets and cool antler for show-and-tell. As I turned back around, I ran right into the back of Scarface again, who had stopped in his tracks to smell the air. Embarrassed, I quickly stepped back but Scarface was too intent on what the air was sharing to care about my lack of attention. Red, too, began to sniff loudly and the hair on both of their backs started to rise. Reflecting back on the last time they got this excited, I began to feel a little uneasy. I couldn't help but notice that we were in a large clearing with no trees around for about a quarter mile in front of us. Off to the right, about a hundred yards away, was a fifty foot solid rock wall that dug into the mountain side and offered no way up or out.

Off to the left, was open field for a mile, with a few shrubs and some movement that was much too far away to distinguish what it might be. Really not wanting to get caught in another battle of tribe member hostility, I felt my chest tighten with anxiety. Red seemed to know exactly what was coming and started to make a move up the trail. Scarface had other ideas and blew out a warning that redirected Red to the rock wall area to our right about a hundred yards away. The distant movement turned out to be the familiar pack of grey wolves from the rock slide. As we moved quickly to the rock face with our backs against the wall it looked like we had nowhere to run to. I guess this meant that we were in for a fight. I knew I could never hope to outrun this pack, let alone fight them.

The wolves came in strong with a rush that abruptly stopped about twenty feet away, with the lead male letting out a low growl. He began stepping back and forth in a nervous movement bringing his head high and low with his lips drawn back showing his brilliant teeth. Red had thrown down the blankets and with an angry growl, brandished his bludgeoning tool in front of him, holding it low. Scarface also brought his fighting tool out in front, holding it low as he switched places with Red to stand on Red's left—they now stood shoulder to shoulder.

It was then I realized Scarface was left handed and Red was right handed, which accounted for the switching of places with such natural movement. I was on Scarface's left, which worked out for me, as I too was left handed. But with the odds facing us, I clutched my hatchet with both hands out in front of me and prepared myself for a difficult battle. I now understood the fast thinking of Scarface as he chose this spot to fight. They could not surround us to attack our flank. Facing off with our backs against the wall made it difficult for the pack and actually left us with the advantage. They would not all rush in at the same time, there simply was not enough room.

The first brave wolf rushed in from the right side as a second one lunged in straight at Scarface. With a quick, well rehearsed blow, Red swung the antler in hard on the side of its head and knocked the first attacker to the ground, rolling him twice before he regained his unsteady footing. Scarface came straight down on top of the head of the second and stopped him hard in the dirt. The wolf fell with his head right at my feet. I chopped down hard onto the top of the skull with the sharp edge of the hatchet. This would be my movement I decided, as the effect from the hatchet was devastating and final. Pleased with myself and gaining a touch of confidence I readied myself for the next possible candidate.

My wait was brief as one of the snarling grey wolves leapt forward with his nose wrinkled up and teeth snapping towards my face. My timing was off as the hatchet glanced off the side of his head only knocking him down and leaving a small gash on the top of his head. Gaining his feet quickly he lunged to his feet with another snap at my face, I felt the wind of an antler flying past my face as it came down with precision force on the center of the skull, opening it wide as the life instantly went out of the canine.

The smell of blood intensified the pack into a more aggressive behavior. The lead male rushed Scarface and the smaller black male moved in low towards me. This time my accuracy was spot on as I brought the black wolf down hard but had trouble removing the sharp instrument from where it had lodged inside the thick, dense skull. The lead male Scarface had struck down was getting a second and final blow when one of the wolves came in over the top of the lead male and sunk his teeth into the right arm of Scarface. Red was just swinging down on his mangy attacker as my hatchet finally came loose. With a wolf locked on Scarface's right arm and an antler in his left hand he tried to swing the antler down onto the head to make it release. Red had just finished off his attacker so he came to the aid of Scarface. Dropping his antler, he reached in with both hands and wrapped his long fingers around the neck of the male that had latched on to Scarface's arm. As Red tightened his grip the wolf let go of Scarface. Red had no intentions of letting go until he had finished his task.

The pack had lost its lead and four others which by my count made a pack of sixteen, a leader-deficient pack of eleven. Even though fierce and deadly, the rest of the pack was more cautious without the brazen example to follow, and they slinked back to a safer distance. We stood poised and ready as the pack circled restless and unsure of their next move. Their heads hung low as they shifted their weight from side to side. It was if they had lost their compass for direction. They couldn't decide if the leader lying on the ground was going to get back up and take charge. I was pleased that they had backed off, but still understood that the threat was not over.

I was standing over the body of a dead wolf; when I foolishly let my guard down to bend over to move it out of the way. As I bent over, one of the wolves perceived this as an opportunity to attack and lunged towards me. It must have thought that since I was smaller than my two companions, I appeared less threatening. Red was much more attentive and jumped in my direction, reaching out with both hands and knocking me to the ground on top of the dead wolf. As the wolf sailed through the air, he was greeted with the wide open hands of Red, as the two came crashing down on top of me. Snapping viciously, the wolf instinctively tried to bite at Red's throat but missed completely, which left his own neck exposed to Red's powerful grip.

I was lying face down on the dead wolf with Red on top of me. Lying on his back,

Red had an angry wolf by the neck firmly gripped in both hands. Scarface struck down hard with his antler on the top of the helpless skull of the wolf ending the chaos. This seemed to take the fight out of the pack as they backed off an even further distance. For the next half hour the remaining ten wolves snapped and fought among themselves. Then they began circling and pacing back and forth until one of the more aggressive wolves took the lead and moved back down the hill from where they had come.

As if unable to stop themselves, they all circled in behind the new self-appointed alpha and loped off into the distance after a few furtive glances at us. With Red and Scarface standing ready with their antlers I had gotten back up from the crushing weight of the smelly red beast and was standing beside them with my own destructive hatchet. Watching them leave was a relief as the distance between us grew. The three of us stood quietly for another ten minutes staring at the last place they disappeared. I knew Red had saved my life in that brief moment. I realized that thanking him and shaking his hand was out of the question. Whether he liked it or not, his protective instincts to protect all members of his tribe had been exposed, I hoped that someday I could repay him.

It was nearly dark by the time we rounded the glacier into the open field towards the cabin. I slowed down at the entrance while the other two walked past, as if I didn't exist. They disappeared out of sight into the opening of their own cave. I was surprised when I stepped into the cabin to discover two freshly tanned hides, one elk and one deer, laid carefully out on my bed. Tired and sore I slipped under the warmth of the two new hides and drifted off into a deep, much needed sleep.

The following morning, Radar and Scarface came up the trail followed by two females who looked small in comparison to Scarface. Both were easily six feet tall and looked every bit of two hundred and fifty pounds each of solid muscle. A third female

followed a little further behind and I recognized her immediately as the female who
had the baby about three weeks previously.

In the light of the day her features were
unlike the rest. She had much smoother skin
and although athletic in build she was very
feminine in her shape. She was an inch or
two shorter than the other two females and
couldn't have weighed more than one hundred and eighty pounds, making her look
even smaller by comparison to the other
two. I couldn't help but notice her face. She
seemed more human than the others and had
a tough beauty to her appearance. With a
strong jaw line and high cheekbones, she
took on the look of an attractive Native
American with short hair.

She must have noticed me staring at her
because she glared at me and stepped in close
behind the two larger females to keep from
my view. Embarrassed that I was gawking,
I backed into the doorway of the cabin and
tried to busy myself with organizing the
few things inside the small room. I didn't

feel right noticing her beauty, but by any-one's standards this female was impressive and actually very attractive in her overall appearance.

They came to the doorway and the two large females waited outside while Radar boldly came inside and stepped past me. He began by picking up my blankets and clothes that were on the bed and passed them out the door to the first female who turned away towards the cave and left. Next he handed the canvas bag containing the wrapped up pistol, old ammo, extra socks and wallet to the second waiting female who turned towards the cave and followed. I stood to the side and watched as Radar gathered up the two deer hides and a few other miscella-neous items and handed them off to the last, smaller female who shot me a curious glance and turned away towards the cave. Then it hit me like a rock—the smaller female had bright blue eyes that made her unique from the rest. The only other member with that brilliant blue eye color was Elder.

I scanned the cabin and it looked abandoned, emptied of anything of interest. Radar had removed any trace of my presence from this building which meant only one thing... I was going to have to stay inside the cave this winter. Meanwhile, Scarface stood just outside the door and looked out over the glacier area as if daydreaming about something, uninterested in what was going on within the cabin.

I followed the three females, along with Radar, toward the mouth of the cave. I found myself fighting the gag reflex as I ducked my head into the low opening. With the females already well into the cave and out of sight, Radar and I worked our way through the opening on the right and out past the water into the back opening. I was surprised to see that brush and pine boughs had been placed over the opening to cover most of the space and block out the wind and weather, as well as much needed ventilation and light.

Radar had me follow him deeper into the opening to the left. We continued past the covered opening, maybe fifty more feet, to yet another entry that afforded a small amount of light high up the wall maybe ten or twelve feet. The light was not direct but somewhat blocked by the contours of the rock. It allowed illumination of the wide open room with eight beds (or nests for lack of a better term). The spaces were mostly pine boughs and small twigs that were round in shape rather than long, similar to a bed that I would make to sleep on.

My belongings were on one of the spaces, along with several of my clothes and blankets. I was located right next to the blue eyed female who sat against the wall nursing her infant. The baby was wrapped up in the shirt I had given her, and I could see the hair on top of his little head growing in thick and black. Lying on her bed were two blankets that I recognized as the two that Red had taken from the campers at the trailhead. I wondered if the baby had any more hair growing on his body like the rest but couldn't tell with him wrapped in the shirt.

Great, I was going to spend the winter months next to a squawking baby. The female rarely took her eyes off me. She seemed unafraid and comfortable with my presence. All of the beds were occupied by other members that I had seen outside from time to time. Several were uninterested in me, but there were a few that showed signs of curiosity and some displayed distrust. It was odd how my life had put me in this situation, and how easily I had gotten comfortable with their lifestyle and simple uncomplicated ways. I actually beginning to enjoy their company and was fascinated by their closeness as a tribe and family.

My first night in the cave was restless. I couldn't believe how loud a room full of snoring giants could be. It will keep a man from sleeping but the echoes and acoustics were amazing. Not once did the infant cry out or make any noise in the night. With 'Blue Eyes' on one side of me and Radar on the other I felt like I was put there on purpose. Perhaps they did that to keep the others from bothering me.

In the morning, I heard the signature sounds of Raspberry in the room and lifted my head to see her on the other side of Radar, kicking at him playfully with her big awkward feet. She didn't seem to care that I was there and even blew her infamous sounds at me when she left the room. Looking over, I saw Blue Eyes facing me on her side in the fetal position with her baby hugged against her chest, her calm blue eyes looking through me. Radar was also looking at me and sat up with that 'let's go' look in his eyes.

Childs Play

The air was crisp and chilly as several members of the tribe moved through the valley floor looking for smaller game to bring back to the rock slide miles away. We had been slowly moving beside a wide fast moving creek that offered several rabbits, as well as a few blue grouse. I contemplated pulling out my fishing line to see if the creek would offer up a few trout to contribute to the bounty.

I noticed Raspberry off on her own with a stick swirling it at the edge of the water. Like a child at play, she enjoyed the reflection in the water and the effects of the stick as it rippled and distorted what she saw. She paralleled what every playing child does, acting carefree and open minded to the wonders of her surroundings. Periodically she would spout off a random "plbbbt" with her tongue, blowing air with almost a smile on her cute little face. As she took it all in, a large tree that had fallen across the water caught her eye and took up her undivided attention. I smiled because I knew she couldn't help herself. She just had to climb on that tree. Drawn to it like a new toy or a slide in a park for a child, she walked to the roots of the tree and awkwardly climbed aboard.

At first she hesitated as the tree moved and flexed from her weight. As she climbed higher towards the narrower, smoother part of the tree, it flexed and bounced providing a more exciting, bouncy ride. Well over the water now, she straddled the tree in a seated position and moved her shoulders and head up and down to make the tree bounce higher. As I watched, I became amused at her innocence and I was enjoying the pleasure she gained from the bouncy ride. The more she bounced the more her teeth showed and for a moment, she was actually smiling with delight. The more she bounced, the more she sounded off with her typical 'Raspberry' sound. I felt like I was seeing a very human side of her as she played and enjoyed herself in her natural habitat. I knew if she saw me watching her she would certainly scowl at me and scold me in her own way. I got up and turned to walk away when I heard the sound of the limbs breaking loose.

Looking back at her I thought the worst case scenario was that she would get a good dunking in the water and be soggy and cold for a bit. The thought of it made me smile, as I watched the tree descend into the water about ten feet below with Raspberry riding her little wooden pony into the chilly bath. At the last two feet of the decent, one of the lower branches plunged into the ground forcing the tree to turn violently to the side. The tree rotated almost a full circle. The branches below the surface spun around taking Raspberry with them and plunging her into the water, pinning her just below the water's surface. I hesitated, thinking she might come to the surface but saw her hand flailing just above the surface, her entire body still pinned below.

The water was deep and kept her submerged. The weight of the tree was too much for her to push and the limb held her tight beneath the surface. Seeing that she was trapped, I jumped into the icy cold water beside her, grabbing the rough surface of the tree, and lifted with all my strength but with no success. Looking down, I could see her face just barely below the surface with her eyes wide with terror. She breathed out in panic and the bubbles rose to the surface only an inch away. I knew that this was her final gasp if we couldn't get her up so I tried one more time. I began to panic and grabbed the tree and pulled with all my might on the branch that held her captive. It wouldn't budge, not one inch. Out from under the water, Raspberry reached her hand out to the front of my shirt and grabbed hold of my arm. Her grip was weak and fading quickly so I did the only thing I could think of. I inhaled deeply and plunged my face below and reached for her lips and blew into her mouth as much air as she would take.

Immediately she blew it back out in surprise and uncertainty, blowing bubbles to the surface. Once again I inhaled deep and forced another breath into her mouth and again she blew it out. This time I inhaled deep and blew into her mouth, followed by forcing my hand over her mouth to make her hold it longer. Just one inch below the surface I could see the look of shock, surprise and confusion in her eyes but she accepted the air quickly and held it for a few seconds.

As I came to the surface again I shouted, "*HELP*"*!* I took in another fresh breath of air and plunged beneath, reaching for the lips of the fragile life below. Again, she accepted the air with hunger and panic, this time holding the air on her own. Again I surfaced and shouted for help. I knew my shouting would certainly get the attention of the others and they would come, but for now, if this young female was going to live, she needed my help and from what I could see, she understood it too.

Each time I surfaced, I shouted loudly and plunged below to give her the life supporting air she desperately needed. Our rhythm came together as she blew out the breath when she knew I was coming in to refill her lungs. Her hand never let go of my arm and her eyes never closed as she stared through the cold water into my face. Even through the distortion of the water moving over her face I could see the gratitude and understanding in her eyes. She knew that I was there to help her.

On one of my surfaces, I saw Radar and Red coming down the embankment towards the water. I continued to breathe air into Raspberry's mouth, as the two stopped at the water's edge and looked blankly at me. They looked clearly unhappy with my noisy shouting. Again I shouted at them, but they just watched me with confusion and irritation. They had no idea that one of their own was just below the surface and needed their help to live. They continued to stand by, just watching me.

Furious, I shouted again and Radar stepped forward into the water and then stopped. He was confused, still not understanding that Raspberry was fighting for her life below. As I brought my face out of the water, I reached up and held out the hand of Raspberry still clinging to my arm. This was all Red needed to see as he plunged into the water towards me. Radar still stood transfixed, not realizing what was happening.

Red reached under the surface and tried to pull on Raspberry's arm to break her free, but I knew the branch would puncture her body if too much force was used trying to free her. I put my hand on Red's large forearm and pulled it away from Raspberry's arm, placed it on the tree itself and pushed as if to lift the tree. Looking curiously at me, he seemed ready to try whatever it was that I had in mind. I held Red still for a moment and plunged another breath of air into the lungs of the helpless female below.

As I came back up, Red knew exactly what to do and we both grabbed the side of the tree pushing it upwards. Moving just a little, it raised but not enough to help. Red barked loudly over his shoulder towards Radar, who immediately rushed into the water to help. Again, I put my hand on Red's forearm to wait, as I pushed my face down to give air to the weakening lungs below. Now with Radar positioned higher up the trunk of the tree, all three of us pushed upwards and the tree moved up roughly three inches. It was just enough for Raspberry's face to surface and gasp a breath of clean air of her own. The weight of the tree was too much for us to hold and it slipped from our grasp forcing her below the surface of the cold water again.

On the bank appeared the old female Grumpy and two other females who were looking curiously at the three of us in the water. A loud series of tones and barks from Red had them all scrambling into the water and grabbing at the tree from all sides. Again, I plunged my face into the water as I saw the bubbles of air rush up to the surface. One more time Raspberry accepted the air with hunger and enthusiasm. Finally, with the help of all five members, the tree rose up about a foot and once again Raspberry's face and head came to the surface gasping for that pure, life sustaining air. Taking the opportunity, I pulled her below the surface again to free her from the stubborn branch that had held her captive. Seeing that Raspberry was free, the five members dropped the heavy tree back into the water.

Exhausted and frightened, Raspberry stood up on her feet beside me. She clung to me with her arms around my neck, shivering from the cold water and burrowed her face into my chest. I was unsure as to whether or not to put my arms around her so I stood still, arms at my side. Grumpy placed her hand on Raspberry's head and turned her towards the bank to the dry ground above. Once out of the water, Raspberry turned and looked back at me. She reached out her hand, grabbed my shirt and pulled me towards the dry bank, not once taking her eyes off of mine. The others all seemed intent on the fact that she had reached out and touched me. The dynamics of my presence and acceptance within their tribe forever changed that day.

Rope Trick

The days seemed to run into weeks as I settled in to the life as a cave dweller. I was able to come and go unescorted through the cave and into my "barracks" that I shared with the others. One night when the temperatures had dropped well below zero I felt a bump on my back as Radar had scooted towards me and was actually up against me with his arm draped over my shoulder. I was wrapped deep under several deer hides and doing just fine when yet another hand came over Radar and dropped on the side of my face. Irritated at first, I realized that they were tightening up for the warmth but I didn't need this nasty hand on my face. Reaching to fling it away, I realized that it was Raspberry's hand and it made me smile.

It was too dark to see anything in this room full of snoring members but it was like one big happy family. Lying on my side, I felt Blue Eyes lift the blankets and start shuffling in close to me with her little infant between us. Now with Radar spooning against my back, Raspberry's dirty hand on my face, the knees of Blue Eyes against my shins, her baby against my chest and her face just inches away from my own I was trapped in this position with my new found family. Listening to the sounds of snoring, feeling the unpleasant breath of Blue Eyes in my face, and accepting a blanket-stealing baby, I smiled broadly and drifted off to sleep.

The next day, several members went out to the high bluffs just above our camp to gather small pine branches and to warm themselves on the rocks. I had just finished using the 'outdoor facilities' when I heard Raspberry let out a primal scream sending Red and Scarface rushing up to the bluffs.

Curious, I came out to the area where the bluff had smaller cliffs protruding well above the opening on the back side of the cave. Just below the outcropping of cliffs, Radar had somehow fallen onto a very small ledge with nowhere to go. His ankle looked swollen from a break or a sprain and his left arm was bleeding from a cut on his forearm. Below him was a sheer six hundred-foot drop to the rocks below. Twenty feet above him were Red and Scarface. Radar was stuck on a small, two foot by four foot ledge that tapered off into thin air. It looked as if he had fallen from the outcropping above. It amazed me how he had landed on such a small space and not fallen the entire distance to his death.

Raspberry looked past Red towards me and immediately came over and grabbed my hand, looking up at me with her big wide pleading eyes. Scarface showed obvious surprise at this outward display of comfort and trust, though Red didn't seem to notice. With Raspberry not letting go of my hand, she led me to the top of the bluff as if it was a better view of the peril that Radar was in. With his chest against the face of the cliff, he turned his face up to me with a look of sheer terror, blood running from a cut on the front of his forearm. He had gotten himself in a very precarious spot.

His position looked grim as I watched Scarface pace from side to side with worry on his furrowed eyebrows. Raspberry was still clinging to my hand, staring up at me. I felt I had better find a solution quickly, especially since Radar was starting to show signs of panic. Then I remembered the long rope I had seen in the open room of the cave and turned to retrieve it.

With Raspberry on my heels, I ran at a pretty good pace towards the cave leaving Red and a puzzled Scarface behind as they watched Raspberry follow me. I knew I needed to hurry seeing the growing panic on

Radar's face. He was unpredictable and not in the right mindset to handle his current situation. I ducked into the cave weaving my way past the water and out into the opening at the rear of the cave. I saw the rope against the wall and quickly picked it up and headed back out to the entrance. Once out in the light, I hurried towards the bluffs. As I ran, I inspected the rope and found it to be old, weathered and in fairly rough shape. I needed to test its reliability for weight before I would trust it with anyone's life. With Raspberry right beside me, I ran towards the bluff to an anxious Scarface and a curious Red.

There was a nice sized tree above the bluff where I was able to tie off the rope a section at a time and test it with my own weight, yanking on it to verify its dependability. I found a section about a quarter of the way through the rope that had been chewed through by small rodents, which only left about thirty five feet of useable rope. It was a good quality rope at one time but had enough age to it that I had a hard time trusting it completely. Given the situation, I had no other choice.

Standing above Radar, I didn't have enough length in the rope to tie it off to the tree for a failsafe. I needed a different anchor point to get myself down to tie Radar to one end of the rope and then somehow hoist him back up to the top without dropping him. I thought of lowering the rope to Radar and wondered if he would know what to do with it, but unless he was tied correctly, we would certainly lose him over the edge. I had a plan but would need a good solid anchor and some much needed help from the others. There was nothing stationary to tie off to, so I recruited the next best thing—Scarface.

Risking it all, I confidently approached Scarface and Red with my rope in hand. As I stopped in front of Scarface he looked cautious and unsure about what to think of my bold approach, but at this point, it was all or nothing. With the rope in my hands, I dropped the whole rope to the ground, except for one end. With exaggerated movements, I tied it securely to my own waist right in front of him. Next, I took the other end and reached out to tie it around Scarface's waist, which evoked a low, deep growl. I stopped for only a second but continued to lean in to reach it around his waist. I couldn't quite reach my arms around him without literally bear hugging him and was relieved when Red took the rope from my hands and passed it through from the other side.

The look that passed from Scarface to Red was of anger, defiance, and noticeable irritation. I continued to tie a knot that would not come undone or easily untied. The next part was going to be tough as I had to get Scarface to sit down and hold the rope. The only thing I could think of was aggressive, so I took hold of the rope at Scarface's waist and pulled towards the edge which immediately made him resist and squat lower. Taking the opportunity, I placed my hand on his shoulder and pushed down with all my strength. Down went Scarface, on his heels and onto his butt. At the same time I squatted down low and pulled on the rope hard as if to lower myself over. Scarface naturally took hold of the rope with both hands and dug his heels in. This was just what I needed for a reliable anchor.

I put my weight into pulling on the rope and trusted that Scarface would not let himself go over the edge and leaning over the bluff I literally put my life into his hands. Red stepped forward and put his hands on the rope to add to the anchor point; another bit of stubborn weight. I felt they both knew I was trying to help Radar but didn't like my methods. However, I trusted their survival instincts to hold tight and not follow me over the edge.

Still tied tightly around my own waist, I held on to the rope and cautiously lowered myself over the edge and out of view from Red and Scarface towards Radar's position, twenty feet below. I came in to his left and carefully watched his movements and hoped that he wouldn't try to leap onto me or panic in some way. Surprisingly enough, he didn't want to move at all and I literally had to force him to shuffle to the side so I could share the ledge with him. Once on the ledge

I found I had an extra three feet of rope at my disposal, so I tied a knot in the rope which offered a nice one foot loop for me to put my arm into for insurance.

With my arm strung through the loop, I kept a good tension on the rope by leaning into it so Scarface would feel the need to hold his position. I delicately untied the rope from my own waist and retied it around terrified and stiff Radar, frozen in his position. I tied it up snug and tight under his arms with the knot in the center of his chest. Tying higher on Radar gave me enough extra rope to put another smaller loop into the rope which I placed one of Radar's rigid arms through and placed his hands on the rope above the knot.

This was the difficult part as the hard climb to the top would be without the safety knot securely tied around my waist. Using my feet to walk the wall I pulled myself up over the top of Radar who still hadn't moved. I covered the twenty foot climb as quickly as I could, until I had pulled myself up into the view of Scarface and Red. As soon as I cleared the top, I immediately started pulling on the rope with all my strength, lifting Radar off his feet and above the security of the ledge.

With a quick yelp of surprise, the loss of footing made him panic, and without the solid surface under his feet, he began to kick frantically. Knowing that it was only a matter of time before he thrashed himself out of the rope, I pulled hard and quickly, which put Scarface and Red into motion as they pulled backwards. Radar was quickly and roughly dragged onto the upper level of the cliff. Scrambling to his feet, he lunged away from the cliffs edge and towards the safety of solid ground, coming to a rest with his back against the tree.

With the strain and weight that had been applied to the rope, I had a difficult time untying the knots as an impatient Scarface waited for me to finish. Raspberry came up and stood between us as I fought with the rope. Her comfort and trust with me didn't go unnoticed with Scarface or the others as she literally leaned against my chest. This was beginning to feel like a family and I wasn't seen as the odd one out. Heading back down to the rock slide, I watched Raspberry wrap her arm around Radar's wrist and walk beside him. In an odd formation Scarface walked beside me with Red following close behind, only this time I was not uncomfortable or out of place. If anything, I felt that I had finally found my place within their family.

Carrying Stones

After a light snow had fallen the evening before, I was surprised at how warm the next day was. I enjoyed the sun as it quickly melted away all the signs of the brief encounter with the upcoming winter. We had all wandered off below the camp into a small grove of trees that offered a small trickle for water and a few flat rocks for sprawling to soak up the heat from the sun high above us. Several members soon tired of the area and eventually headed back up the hill, towards the entrance about a mile away.

Looking around I saw Raspberry in a tree about ten feet up plucking pine cones and dropping them on Radar who was on the flat rocks below trying to sun himself on this warm, lazy day. A little further away, I saw Blue Eyes sitting with her back to me cradling her young baby along with Grumpy who had started to warm up to me a little over the past few weeks. Scarface was close by with his antler in hand wandering aimlessly through the grove of trees looking out over the vast range in front of us with a faraway look. After a few minutes of reminiscing, Scarface turned towards the cave and slowly made his way up the hill stopping here and there to pick at something in the dirt or to sniff the air.

Blue Eyes had gotten more comfortable with me and preferred to have me close as she turned around to look at me with her piercing blue eyes. Never turning her gaze away, as if waiting for me to get up, I finally took the hint and wandered over to where she and Grumpy were sitting and plopped down beside Blue Eyes. I smiled to myself as I realized that she had finally trained me, and all it took was a long patient stare from those big blue eyes to get me to do what she wanted. As if on cue she leaned heavily against my side and forced me to have to reposition with my back to her so she could have a proper leaning post. Blue Eyes had given me the job of become her leaning post companion and seemed to take comfort in my presence. Grumpy stood up, reached out and gently took the infant from Blue Eyes and walked away towards the camp, leaving the two of us on the flat surface of the stone.

It looked as if the younger female had a trusted babysitter and was going to have proper help raising her baby. Sitting there with my back to Blue Eyes, I watched as Grumpy made her way up the hill and out of sight at the base of the slide. Looking just a few feet away, I saw Radar on his back attempting to throw pine cones straight up towards Raspberry only to find that they made their way straight back to him which was visibly irritating to Radar. It was perfect weather with virtually no wind. The four of us that remained in the grove had become close, like family, without a care in the world. I felt Blue Eyes back straighten up and without a sound she leapt to her feet, leaving me almost flat without her opposing weight.

She blew out a loud hiss which got the attention of Radar who scrambled to his feet. I started to follow Blue Eyes and watched as she quickly moved towards the trees, reached up for the lower hanging branches and easily pulled up and out of sight. Recognizing this as the first defense system of the tribe, I ran to a nearby tree and also hoisted myself upwards. I was in the tree next to the one already occupied by Raspberry and Radar, who had climbed a good twenty feet up. I climbed quickly as I reached a safe distance of about twenty feet also and was eye level with Radar who was perched a few feet below Raspberry. Off to my right, not more than thirty feet, was Blue Eyes sitting with her chest against the tree in a bear hug fashion, looking intently out over the open field below the grove.

I heard an excited yelp and another bark as I saw a pack of eight wolves come into view. They might have been the pack that we had encountered before, minus a couple since the fight at the rock wall. They were mangy and thin with the same nervous pacing, back and forth with their heads held low, looking mean as ever. I knew they had our scent but didn't have a fix on our location and might very well pass on by.

I looked across at Blue Eyes who had her gaze fixed on the pack. She was tense and rigid with her knuckles showing white from her grip on the tree. Looking over at Radar, I noticed his eyes were on me, wide with fear. His hands were also gripped tightly around the tree he has holding. Above him, I looked up towards Raspberry and saw she didn't like the idea of being so far away from Radar and was easing herself in a position to descend next to her protector.

The branch she stood upon snapped free and the upper branch she had used for balance was too weak to support her weight.

She screamed as she dropped through the branches, tumbling over and hitting her head against the tree several times on the way to the rocks below.

As she fell, one of the lower tree branches she had used to climb to the top had caught her just under her jaw bone. It tore through the flesh from her jaw line to the upper side of her cheekbone, spinning her in a summersault as hit the ground feet first. The twenty-foot fall to the rocks came with devastating consequences. Her right ankle rolled under her weight and broke with bone piercing through the skin. Her jaw began to bleed profusely as she desperately tried to get to her feet. Her broken ankle made it hard to stand and she cradled her left hand as if it were injured also. Leaning against the base of the tree and unable to put any pressure on her right foot Raspberry reached upwards for the lower branches that were close to four feet away. She was in no condition to jump, and having only one hand to pull herself up, she could not climb back up to safety.

Radar sprung into action and lowered himself to her aid. The scream, combined with the noise of branches snapping, was just what the pack of wolves needed to locate their prey. As they locked in on her location, the smell of fresh blood only fueled the excitement of the wolves, and they came loping towards the tree. As Radar came down the branches, my adrenaline kicked in and I began to descend from my elevated position to come to Raspberry's aid. Blue Eyes hissed loudly as she descended down the tree and landed on the soft earth below. The wolves were already within five feet of Raspberry, who blew loudly and hissed, baring her white teeth with a frightening display.

Unable to fight, she still lunged, full of courage at the closest wolf which made him shy backwards. Just then a silver male sprang forward and snapped a piece of skin from her left arm. Throwing her head back, Raspberry screamed a loud primal howl that sent shivers down my spine as I dropped to the ground below. Radar let go of the last branch and landed on the male that had its jaws locked on Raspberry. He wrapped his hands around the neck of the frantic wolf and applied his bore down with pressure. Even though I was closer, I was outrun by Blue Eyes as she lunged in to the aid of the others. In an instant, another wolf pounced in and sunk his teeth into Raspberry's shoulder and pulled her to the ground. Not letting go he began to violently shake his head from side to side.

Blue Eyes attacked and jumped on his back digging her strong fingers into the neck and sank her teeth into the side of the face of the jaws that had Raspberry held captive. I came in from the backside of Raspberry and tried to get my hands on her to pull her away from the teeth as they were being pried apart. As the wolf succumbed to Radars chokehold, another male came in and sank his teeth into his left hip. Blue Eyes finally succeeded in pulling the mouth apart enough for me to pull the helpless young female free and closer to the tree but the wolves had tasted blood and they were determined to move in for the kill. As Blue Eyes released her grip, the wolf turned quickly and lunged at her with razor sharp teeth and locked in on her shoulder, just missing the throat.

With Blue Eyes fighting off the wolf locked on her shoulder, I glanced over at Radar who was fighting the wolf that had latched onto his hip. I watched as a second one jumped in and sank his teeth into Radar's forearm pulling backwards with quick jerking movements. Pulling Raspberry onto my chest, I dug in with my heels and put my back against the tree holding Raspberry in front of me. A large grey female lunged in and buried her teeth into Raspberry's left thigh and began to pull violently backwards. As Raspberry let out another loud shrill scream, I instinctively reached out with my hands to grab the female wolf's head. I was met by yet another one of the pack that came in low to my left and sank his teeth deep into my ribs under my outstretched arms.

Feeling his teeth sink in was not as awful as the violent shaking of his head, as I felt the flesh begin to tear away from my ribcage. I got my hands on the neck of the female wolf and sunk my right thumb deep into the side of its opened mouth while the other thumb quickly searched for the eye opening of the snarling female. As if in slow motion, I felt Raspberry's hands slide down my arms as she tried with all her might to grip the neck of the large female. Her fingers trembling she ducked her head down and sank her teeth into the soft fleshy nose of the grey female that had her thigh.

A third pack member rushed in and sank his teeth into Raspberry's right shoulder and started pulling to the side violently shaking in a backwards direction. I heard the crunch as the teeth went beyond the flesh and deep into the shoulder of my fragile companion. Not letting go with her left hand, Raspberry began to weaken quickly and her small little body was giving out fast. Even though she was being pulled in two directions, Raspberry was still fighting, bearing down with her teeth on the nose of the larger female wolf and growling fiercely in the face of the female.

In a flash I saw Red, Scarface and Grumpy show up out of nowhere as they brandished their tools of destruction. Red came down hard on the wolf that had Blue Eyes by the shoulder, making short work of him with a powerful deadly blow to the top of his head. Scarface devoted his first blow to the large grey female wolf that had Raspberry's thigh and with two sharp powerful blasts quickly finished the female. Grumpy literally jumped onto the back of the second wolf that had Raspberry's shoulder, wrapped her hands around its neck and initiated a powerful grip that immediately stopped the air flow from the attacker. She continued the incredible pressure until the heart stopped as well.

Red turned his attention to one of the two wolves that had Radar and brought down a terrible blow to the skull of the wolf attached to Radar's hip. The second wolf, not liking the odds, lost his courage quickly and let go of Radar's forearm, slinking backwards. It was Blue Eyes who stepped over Raspberry and me to contend with the angry grey wolf that had me by the ribs. In one smooth movement she dropped her knees into the raised back of the wolf and reached under his neck and began to roll the head backwards. As it let go of my side, Blue Eyes continued to kneel down with her body weight and pull back, literally bending the body backwards until it snapped the stubborn spine beneath the sinewy flesh.

With only two wolves left, the attack was over as they moved back fifty yards and watched nervously, waiting for the six others to join them. With Raspberry still sitting against my chest, I could hear her weak, hoarse breathing as she coughed and relaxed into me. She wrapped her hand around my arm and pulled it close to her chest and buried her face into my shoulder. Looking down, I could see her left thigh was bleeding heavily and her ankle was turned at a very ugly angle. With her hand on my arm she breathed out a sound with every exhale that was of pain and sadness. Her left hand began to tremble as she drew me closer and tried to move her right hand but the shoulder wouldn't allow it. Standing over us was Red, Scarface and the older female quietly looking down, helpless to do anything for Raspberry. Leaning against me with her chin on my shoulder was Blue Eyes. Radar limped in and slumped down resting his weary head on the right thigh of Raspberry, looking up into her weary face.

The heart breaking scene was unbearable as Raspberry began to uncontrollably twitch throughout her little fragile body. Looking up at me with the wolf's blood on the sides of her face, I realized that Raspberry had fought bravely to the bitter end. Her left hand began to pat lightly on my shoulder, as if tapping out the final heart beats that she had left within her. Trying to be strong, I couldn't choke back the tears as the first rolled down my face onto her little shoulder. Reaching up, she touched the second tear as it fell from my eye and rolled down my face, closing her fingers to feel its moisture. Again, she began to tap out the rhythm on my arm but as her breathing slowed, her tiny fingers lost the strength to continue.

Her tapping finally stopped altogether followed by her breathing.

Looking up, I didn't have to let the others know what had just taken place as the look on their faces was obvious. Unlike the death of the male where the others stayed calm and quiet, I saw tears streaming from the eyes of Scarface as he looked in horror at the lifeless little female in my arms. Red turned his bloodshot eyes down and stepped away pounding his fist into his own chest as if to drive out the pain in his heart. Blue Eyes sat still with her tears running down my shoulder and onto my chest. Radar just clung to Raspberry's leg and sobbed uncontrollably.

It was the old female that first broke the silence with an ear shattering howl that made the most sorrowful, frightening echo through the mountain range. Her explosive cry out to the sky was perfect for the moment as it lasted and lingered heavily on the air. I looked around and saw almost everyone from the tribe standing around with different tools, antlers, and sticks. One male held an antler and my hatchet that I expect he would have handed off to me if the opportunity had presented itself.

When Raspberry first howled, it had gotten the attention of everyone in the cave and they were all prepared to protect family and members in need. In the tragedy of the situation Raspberry had shown me the beautiful side of the tribe—the closeness, loyalty and compassion for everyone within their family. Scarface leaned down and picked up the limp body of their little Raspberry from my arms and stepped away towards the hill and cave beyond. Radar limped in behind and Blue Eyes helped me to my feet and followed closely behind as we climbed up the open hill side.

By the time we arrived at the cave entrance, Radar was the only one that went inside while all the others lined up on the rocks in the slide. Elder waited on the flat stone as Scarface waited by the entrance for Radar to return. He emerged from the entrance with the deer hide that he had given Raspberry.

He stopped in front of Scarface and placed the blanket over her as if to hide the horrible catastrophe that had happened to their most innocent family member.

I stood in the grass as I had before, and Radar took his place in the ranks with the others in the slide area. Scarface blew out his air and barked out a couple of abrupt tones that got Blue Eyes attention. She immediately came off the slide towards Scarface then past him out to the grassy area where she gently took my hand and led me up to the slide to stand beside her. This seemed to satisfy them as Elder stepped down from the flat stone and Scarface stepped up and in his place.

Facing the entire tribe, Scarface trembled as he looked down at the now lifeless female in his arms. After a short pause he looked skyward and cried out a tremendous agonizing howl that sent shivers up and down my spine. He again looked at the tribe with sad bloodshot eyes, let out a small bark and another long lonely howl that thundered throughout the valley below. Before his tone ended, the older female let out her howl followed by Red, Blue Eyes and several other members of the tribe. It was the saddest thing that I have ever experienced in my life. I was unashamed as my eyes welled up and the tears streamed down my face. As the last member finished his lonesome howl, the tribe again became silent and waited for the final go ahead from Scarface.

With a weak blow from his trembling lips the tribe began methodically picking up rocks one by one and placing them in the grassy area. Staying by Blue Eyes, she handed me the first stone to carry, picked up her own and led the way back and forth to the grassy area. My acceptance was clear and my probation period seemed to be behind me, as Red even gently placed his giant hand on the back of my neck as I passed by.

Once the entire area was cleared of rocks I saw again the male that had been placed there earlier and the boots and pants of the human remains. The tribe lined up for their last touch of the passing member before the actual burial. Scarface came down off the flat rock and stood in front of me and Blue Eyes. Looking down at the covered Raspberry in his arms he presented her to me and laid her in my arms. He walked right beside me as I carried her among the members as they reached out to her.

At the final resting place, Scarface took the feet of Raspberry and together we placed her beside the young male from the last funeral. I stepped back and watched as Scarface placed his hand on her small head for a second before standing up and turning away to leave. Remarkably, Scarface went out to the rock pile and picked up the first stone and handed it to me, picked up a second stone and handed it to Red. He gave a third to Radar and then picked up his own stone. We filed in and placed them around the small body.

Within two hours the slide was as it had always looked and the tribe disappeared inside except for me, Red, Radar and

Scarface. The four of us sat silently in the grass and looked back at the slide, physically and mentally exhausted. All deep within our own thoughts, I wondered where each of us was at mentally. Did they actually process the loss of a loved one like humans or are the memories lost with the setting sun? I felt the loss deep within my chest and judging by the looks on the faces of the others, I believed that they too mourned the loss in their hearts. Standing up I knew I needed to attend to my wounds as I headed towards the glacier for water. The other three stood up and moved quietly towards the cave opening. The night was finally upon us and all needed rest.

Tough choice

With a good foot and a half of snow Scarface and Red decided that we were going to head out for another hunt. I had gotten used to their pattern of hunting which was to go out when the snow was coming in. We would be a few hours at best, searching for mule deer and would always come back the same day with the heavy snow on our heels to completely cover our tracks. We climbed down from our base towards the valley below and circled through some rugged territory. We came upon some open areas with intermittent patches of trees for cover and also deer beds that had provided mule deer bounty in the past. My two towering hunting buddies were just ahead of me when suddenly they dashed into the trees with their antlers poised for the kill.

Feeling sluggish by comparison and surrendering to the fact that I couldn't outrun a spooked deer, I simply stopped by a medium sized tree. Resting, I waited for the telltale thumps on the tree to see what had been brought down. Leaning against the tree with my hatchet in hand, I looked at it in disdain. It was more of a nuisance than hunting tool since I never chased anything down with it. I'd only used it on the wolves that had attacked me.

A little mule deer came up the hill straight towards me at a dead run with its tongue hanging out, laboring against the snow and the incline of the hillside. It was heading straight for me, more intent on escaping the hunter behind, rather than noticing me standing camouflaged against the tree. I tend to believe that it simply didn't see me and was desperately trying to get away. Now was my chance to prove that I too could hunt and bring down deer and provide meat for the tribe. Raising my hatchet slowly, with both hands above my head, I waited for that precise moment to strike. My adrenaline pumping at full speed, I held out for that split second when the deer was right at my feet and swung down with expert skill using all my strength.

As my hatchet flew down with lightning speed, it dawned on me that my limited capacity to bring the hatchet down was slow in comparison to the deer's speed. The deer saw me in plenty of time to veer off to its right leaving me alone, with a whistling hatchet plunging down into the white fluffy snow, bringing me with it as the force was intended to be met at about the three foot line. The momentum of the full strength, downward swinging motion combined with the unsteady footing and steep grade of the hill was too much for me to stop a self inflicted whitewash, face first into the snow.

I didn't have the common sense to let go. With one hand to brace against the fall, I simply clutched the hatchet with both hands and followed it straight into the snow. The sharp edge of the hatchet sliced smoothly into the snow where it abruptly halted its descent into the frozen ground beneath. Unfortunately my face was still moving downward as my left eyebrow came to rest heavily on the flat surface of the back of the hatchet. There was a quick flash of light as I knew that I hit hard but for some reason I jumped back up as quickly as I could, scanning the area to see if anyone had seen my graceful display. With my present company, I knew that they wouldn't care, but instinctively I felt the quicker that I got up the less humiliation I would have to face. I was embarrassed at my clumsy and awkward actions and was relieved that no one was in sight to witness my failed attempt, not even the elusive mule deer.

Reaching up, I gingerly touched my forehead and felt the slick blood from a two inch split above my left eye. A bump the size of a goose egg had already surfaced and there was blood running down the side of my face. I grabbed a fist full of snow and held it on the wound for a minute which melted quickly with the blood. Several more scoops of snow helped the swelling and I finally got the bleeding under control. Then I heard the sound of two thumps about a hundred yards away. I returned two thumps and scooping up another fist full of snow I held it to my head. Covering up the bright red blood in the snow with fresh white powder, I quickly made my way down the hill. With the bleeding stopped, I approached Red and Scarface who were standing together with two large mule deer.

Scarface seemed occupied with his deer and bringing it up to his shoulders for the journey home, but Red couldn't take his eyes off of my forehead. There was almost a smirk on his face and his eyes even looked like he was humored at the ridiculous sight. Scarface looked at Red who still hadn't picked up his deer, and seeing that he was staring at me, turned to look at my face. Quickly, Scarface looked away and turned his body away, putting the deer on his shoulders between us, but not before his face mirrored the same humored smirk that Red had. Without question the two were laughing at me. I couldn't hear it but I saw it on their faces as Red picked up his fresh kill and headed up the hillside.

We had gone maybe two miles towards camp, with two more hours to go when Scarface and Red lunged into a thicket and dropped both deer. Red grabbed me by the waist and hoisted me like a child up to the lower branches of a large tree and gestured for me to go up. Turning he ran to another tree maybe twenty yards away and disappeared high in its branches. Scarface had continued on further away and was nowhere to be seen. About a half mile away, I saw two figures outlined in the snow. They were on the trail that would pass below our position about a hundred yards away. I figured they were hunters but I hadn't seen too many this far back in the woods.

From a distance I could see the two men approaching on snow shoes. My breath caught in my throat as I immediately recognized the way they walked, especially the way the leader was ambling through the snow with a carefree gait. It was my father and his buddy Jeff! I fought hard to stay quiet and stood still, choking back my emotions as I watched them pass quietly by. Giving up our location could have consequences that I certainly could not risk. I had no intentions of giving up this tribe, even accepting the burden of breaking my own heart.

Knowing my father was looking for me was heartbreaking and made me emotionally proud. What I know about my father is that he will never quit his search until he has answers that satisfy his mission. Letting the two men trudge off into the distance was one of the most difficult decisions in my life. I knew that the chance of them discovering my location was virtually impossible. I also knew with a certainty that my father felt I was still alive and that I would have survived in the woods under most any kind of condition. After all, it was his mentoring and training that taught me how to make it in these elements. I was so proud of him for believing in me and continuing to search, but was also burdened with the heavy sadness of what I'm sure was mental torment for him, wondering if his son was safe and alive.

After waiting about twenty five minutes I heard the two methodical thumps on the base of a tree in the distance and returned my own two thumps and began my decent to the ground below. With my throat choking with emotion, I moved quietly up the hillside to where Red and Scarface awaited. With the snow starting to fall and the wind picking up to cover our tracks, we moved out at a fast pace. I was glad my two companions had their backs to me as I had to emotionally process what I had just witnessed. I had chosen the tribe over my own flesh and blood. This was originally not my choice, but with my involvement and the closeness I had developed with this tribe, it was my only option for now.

Unwavering Faith

It was the end of November and several heavy snows had come through and covered the mountains with white frozen powder. The terrain was completely changed and new dangers of snow slides and frostbite were factors to be considered when traveling the high country. Another storm was brewing and it looked to be a long drawn out storm with plenty of accumulation and wind that would make for a difficult passage. The sound of the wind cutting through the trees made a lonely howling sound as it passed through.

The unforgiving weather would not stop and the wind would not wait. The temperatures would not be above freezing again for several months. Through the cold bitter wind, a lone man crested the summit on snowshoes. He was tired, winded and exhausted but as he looked out over the vast treacherous range in front of him he whispered, "I'm not going to stop searching until I have found my son…"

Made in the USA
Middletown, DE
08 March 2024

51041980R00146